"We're in the middle of a lesson," Miss Jespersen called out.

"Come in!" I yelled at the same time, desperate for an interruption.

The door opened, and the hottie from the parking lot walked in.

Up close, he looked even better. His dark hair flopped over his left eye, his black jeans had a hole in the right knee, his T-shirt had a sweet cartoon of the band JamieX on the front, and there was a small tattoo peeking out from under his right sleeve. He was so not the kind of guy who belonged at the uptight Mueller-Fordham School of Music, but here he was. Barging into *my* piano lesson.

This *rocked*.

XOXOXOX

Read all the FIRST KISSES books:

Trust Me by Rachel Hawthorne

The Boyfriend Trick by Stephie Davis

FIRST KISSES

The *Boyfriend*
Trick

Stephie Davis

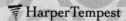
HarperTempest
An Imprint of HarperCollins*Publishers*

HarperTempest is an imprint of
HarperCollins Publishers.

www.harperteen.com

Library of Congress Catalog Card Number:
2006928093
   ISBN-10: 0-06-114309-X
   ISBN-13: 978-0-06-114309-0

Typography by Andrea Vandergrift
❖
First HarperTempest edition, 2007

To my parents, who taught me to follow my
dreams and be true to myself

XOXOXOXO

ACKNOWLEDGMENTS

Thank you to Jackie Fitch and Delilah Ahrendt for being my technical readers on all things piano and music. Any mistakes are mine and mine alone. As always, heartfelt thanks to my wonderful agent Michelle Grajkowski, whose vision and enthusiasm creates opportunities I never would have had without her. And thanks to Leann Heywood for offering me this great opportunity. I miss you! And to Lexa Hillyer and Daniel Ehrenhaft for coming in at the last minute and helping to put the finishing touches on this manuscript. And thank you to my amazing family, whose unwavering support is a treasure. I love you all!

The Boyfriend Trick

Chapter One

XOXOX

I was in the middle of my sixth rendition of Chopin's Nocturne Opus No. 9 when a guy caught my eye as he jogged across the parking lot of the Mueller-Fordham School of Music. I stopped practicing the piano so I could watch his dark hair flutter in his face as he ran, his body lean in his jeans and T-shirt. He wasn't just cute; he was hot with an attitude. In other words: so unlike the other two hundred students at Mueller-Fordham, home of some of the geekiest musical prodigies in the greater Boston area.

After spring break, I was seriously afraid that included me. Geek, that is. Not prodigy. Not anymore.

He disappeared around the corner, and I laid my forearm across the piano keys to compare colors. My skin was the same shade as the ivory. I sighed. How could I finish my freshman year in high school like this? My arms were going to be a dead giveaway that I'd had no life this vacation.

Spending two weeks on a tour of New England with my piano teacher and six other students from the Mueller-Fordham School of Music was a form of torture that should be reserved for serial killers and people who wear ribbon barrettes.

"Good afternoon, Lily." My piano teacher, who I'd dubbed Crusty, strode into the private practice room before I could dive under the piano and hide. The rest of the world called her Miss Jespersen. Not Ms. Not Mrs. *Miss*. As in, *I'm, like, one hundred years old and still unmarried because I'm so evil that I suck the life out of any man who comes near me.*

She eyed me, as if she could see the sparkly purple toenail polish hidden under my sensible and completely unfashionable pianist-worthy shoes. I tried to breathe through my mouth, but I still caught a whiff of mothballs.

Yeah, this was the way to spend my last day of spring break, hanging out with Miss Jespersen instead of at the pool with my friends, checking out guys. Lucky me. According to my parents, being a piano prodigy was a gift. After three years of working with Crusty, it was a gift I was ready to give back.

She waved a newspaper past my face, too quickly for me to see what it said. "You got a review from your recital in Rhode Island last weekend, along with a photo."

"Really?" I snatched the clipping from her hand, then gagged at the picture: my ugly corduroy dress with the white lace collar . . . and my nose. It looked enormous. And my bun was total old lady style. My gut sank as I saw my name in the caption beneath the photo, spelled correctly and everything. They even got my hometown of Westway, Massachusetts, correct. "What paper is this?" *Please tell me it's the monthly bulletin from the nursing home where I'd performed.*

"*The Boston Globe.*"

"*The Globe?*" I croaked, horror welling over me in cold lumps of misery. "As in, circulation seventy gazillion? As in, delivered to the doorstep of every single house in the state the day before school starts up again?" What if my friends saw this photo? They would totally disown me!

Miss Jespersen picked up the clipping and read from it. "With some more experience, Lily Gardner has the potential to develop into a fine musician several years down the road." She set the paper down on the piano and sighed. "Lily, we've been working too hard for you to get lackluster reviews like this. A year ago, every review proclaimed you an immediate star. Now you're reduced to having *potential.*"

I bit my lower lip. "It's not as bad as my picture, at least."

"Your audition is in three weeks, but your

performance has been declining over the last few months."

I felt myself tense up at the mention of that stupid audition. According to Crusty, if I didn't make it into the secondary school program at the NorthEast Seminary of Music, my piano career would be over. Forever. As would my life. This was my chance to ensure my future, and I was blowing it. If that photo hadn't destroyed my future already, of course.

Personally, I was afraid that making it *into* the program would be the final blow to my life. Starting next year, I'd have to spend four to six hours a day there after school, and all day on the weekends. My social life was bad enough now, but if I made it into the NESM program, it would be dead. The thought of never spending another minute with my friends outside of classes made me sick, and I didn't know what to do about it.

Miss Jespersen tapped the piano to get my attention. "There's no passion in your music anymore and without it, you'll fail at the audition. You don't want that, do you?"

I barely resisted the urge to cover my ears and block her out. "I'm not *trying* to fail," I said. "I'm trying to play. I'm just so tired."

"A top performer doesn't let something like exhaustion stop her." She propped the picture of freakazoid me on the piano, so I had to stare at my ugly mug. The cruelest form of torture—next to the two weeks I'd spent on tour, of course. "If I don't see some improvement in the next week, we'll need to think about holding you out of classes until the audition so you can devote yourself to—"

"No!" The only thing keeping me going was the promise of getting back to school and hanging with my friends. "I can handle school and piano, I promise." I would go insane if she made me spend 24/7 trapped in a room with her for the next three weeks. "I swear, Miss Jespersen. I can do both. I promise."

She smiled and nodded approvingly. "That's the kind of passion I like to see. Put it into your music and we won't need to talk to your mom about school."

I shuddered at the thought of her suggesting

anything like that to my mom. Since Crusty had spotted me at an audition when I was eleven, my mom had fallen under her evil spell. I was my mom's chance to be the piano prodigy that she'd never managed to be. She loaded the guilt on all the time about the opportunities I had that she would have killed for, and Miss Jespersen played on that big-time. Even my dad's attempts to keep them reined in weren't always enough.

"Okay, then, let's get to work. Make the walls of this room tremble with emotion."

"Oh, sure. No problem." I stared at the sheet music, rested my fingers on the keys, and all I wanted to do was cry. Instead I lifted my chin and started to play. I could feel Crusty's disappointment after I'd played only three bars and I was about to stop when a light knock sounded on the door.

"We're in the middle of a lesson," Miss Jespersen called out.

"Come in!" I yelled at the same time, desperate for an interruption.

The door opened, and the hottie from the

parking lot walked in.

Up close, he looked even better. His dark hair flopped over his left eye, his black jeans had a hole in the right knee, his T-shirt had a sweet cartoon of the band JamieX on the front of it, and there was a small tattoo peeking out from under his right sleeve. He was so not the kind of guy who belonged at the uptight Mueller-Fordham School of Music, but here he was. Barging in on *my* piano lesson. This *rocked*.

He tossed a careless smile in our direction. "Sorry to interrupt, but I need to grab a few chairs."

Omigosh. He wasn't afraid of her at all. I sat up straighter and checked him out more closely. Who was he?

Crusty drummed her fingers on the piano top. "Just be quick, Rafe."

Rafe? Totally hot name. I bet he'd never worn a tie in his life. I sighed and leaned on the piano as he hoisted four chairs as if they weighed nothing. Cute *and* strong. And he had to be at least sixteen. And he was at *my* music school.

"Rafe? Are you coming or what?"

I jerked my head toward the door as a girl strode in. Her chest was huge, her shirt was, like, twenty sizes too small, her hair was long and highlighted, and she was gorgeous. I grabbed my photo off the piano and shoved it under my butt.

Rafe grinned at her. Not the careless smile we'd gotten, but a real smile, one that made his green eyes crinkle. "Can you grab two music stands, Angel? I've got the rest of the stuff."

Angel? As in her real name, or as in his cute little pet name for her? I decided I didn't like her.

"Keep it quiet, please." Crusty tapped the sheet music in front of me. "Ignore them, Lily."

I gaped at her as Rafe and Angel clanged stands together, making Angel giggle and whisper to Rafe to be quiet. As if I was going to play boring classical music in front of *them*. They practically oozed attitude, and I was so not going to humiliate myself. I mean, it was bad enough that I was wearing Crusty-approved attire and was sitting on a horrific photo of myself. Playing Chopin would be a kiss of death I'd never recover from.

"Lily. Play." Crusty pinned me with a glare and I crumbled.

This was too embarrassing. *Please let him suddenly go deaf.* I felt my cheeks heat up as I started to play. Rafe glanced over at me, and my fingers stuttered. One dark eyebrow lifted, and I forgot to keep going. I simply stared at him.

Crusty cleared her throat, and a small smile curved Rafe's lips. "Go ahead, *Lily*," he said.

"You . . . know me?" Oh, *no*. Had he seen my photo in the paper today?

"Your teacher just said your name."

Relief rushed through me and I almost felt dizzy. *He hasn't seen the picture in the* Globe.

He readjusted one of the chairs that was resting on his shoulder. "Don't let us stop you."

There was something slightly mocking in his tone, but there was something else, too. Something that made my belly go all warm and made goosebumps pop up on my arms.

"Come on, Rafe." Angel brushed past him,

her shoulder intentionally knocking against his, like she wanted me to know that he was hers to touch. "Let's go."

"Right behind you." He gave me a final, speculative look that had my fingers tingling, then he turned and walked out, yanking the door shut behind him with his foot.

I sighed, then Crusty tapped my sheet music. "Play."

The warmth vanished from my body. But I started to play.

Crusty sat silent for almost a whole minute, then she shook her head and stood up. She walked out, slamming the door shut behind her.

I stared at the closed door in shock. She'd never pulled that one on me before.

She probably wanted to punish me by making me sit alone for ten minutes, contemplating all the ways that I was a failure and was letting her and my parents down.

And then I was probably supposed to start practicing so when she came back I could prove I was worthy.

I could do that. Or I could live up to my

mom's constant complaints that I don't always conduct myself in a manner befitting a piano prodigy. . . .

It took me all of five seconds to grab my music off the piano, shove it in my backpack, and climb out the window.

Chapter Two

XOXOX

eased myself into the flowerbeds, landing softly on the mulch and a couple of flowers, listening for Crusty coming after me.

No sound of incoming psycho music teacher.

I slung my backpack over my shoulder, then started walking toward the back of the redbrick house that had been converted into a music school seventy years ago. I'd hang out in the garden area until it was time for my mom to pick me up. No way was I waiting out front where Crusty would be able to find me.

I rounded the corner and then stopped as I

heard voices coming out an open window. One of them was a male voice that made the hair on the back of my neck stand up. *Rafe*.

Anticipation whirling through me, I picked my way around the well-manicured bushes beneath the window and hid under the sill.

I could hear Rafe, Angel, and a couple other voices, all guys. They were arguing about something, but I couldn't tell what. I let Rafe's deep voice drift over me and chase all the Crusty poison out of my system.

But when I heard them mention something about a keyboard, I couldn't resist. I set my backpack on the ground and carefully peeked over the windowsill in true spy fashion.

Rafe was sitting behind a set of drums, Angel had an electric guitar slung over her shoulder, and two other guys dressed in jeans and T-shirts had their backs to me.

One of the guys was tuning an electric guitar, and the other had a microphone in his hand. An unattended electric keyboard was sitting in the corner. They were a band! I bet *they* didn't have to play Chopin. . . .

After a couple minutes, I realized they were arguing about whether to start without the missing keyboard player. Rafe was insistent they should wait, and Angel was complaining that Paige was always late and she was tired of it.

The singer finally told everyone to be quiet and play.

So cool!

When they hit the first note, I nearly died. They were playing the new JamieX song! I listened to it on my iPod every night while I was doing homework.

I sat down in the dirt and leaned against the cool brick, letting the edgy sound wash over me. Yeah, it was a little lacking without the keyboard and the lead singer wasn't exactly in the same class as JamieX, but it was still awesome. Especially in comparison to the classical sheet music in my backpack.

I closed my eyes. The beat of Rafe's drums pounded through my body, my chest vibrating as I sang along. I could sit here for hours and almost forget that there was a freaky piano teacher after me.

The music stopped, and reality came rushing back.

"Our music is too keyboard-intensive to do it without Paige," Angel said. "This is a waste of our time and I'm going home—"

"No!" I jumped to my feet and threw my backpack through the open window before I even knew what I was doing. I heard a crash and then I set my palms on the windowsill and hoisted myself up. "I'll play. Don't stop."

All of them stared at me as I fell over the windowsill and did a face-plant onto the floor. I immediately hopped up and faced the room. Total silence. Great. Lily the social klutz strikes again.

Rafe's cymbal was on the floor, smashed under my backpack. Oops. "Sorry." I kicked my backpack aside, righted the cymbal, and turned toward the group. "So, I'll play keyboard for you."

"Who *are* you?" the singer asked.

"Lily Gardner, child prodigy on my good days, hopeless piece of dirt on my bad ones."

Donning the confident attitude that I usually saved for recitals, I strode over to the keyboard and peered at it. "So, um, where's the *on* switch?" I'd messed around with keyboards plenty of times when I'd stumbled across an unattended one at recitals or in the music school. I could play it no problem, as long as I didn't mess with the synthesizer part.

Rafe hadn't said a word. He was simply staring at me. So I ignored him. A hot guy is one thing. Depriving me of JamieX is another. That trumped everything else.

"I know you. You were just taking the lesson with Rafe's aunt," Angel said. "You play classical and you aren't even very good."

I shot a surprised look at Rafe. "You're related to Crusty?"

The corner of Rafe's mouth twitched. "You call her Crusty?"

"Old Crusty is her full name. Crusty for short." I hesitated. "Um, do you like her? Because if you do, then I was talking about someone else—"

"Can you play?" the singer interrupted.

"If someone would turn this thing on for me." Gah. Did I sound like a dork or what? What loser couldn't find a power switch?

"I'm Chris. The band's called Mass Attack." He walked over and flicked the switch on the far left of the keyboard.

Duh. It had been right in front of me. "I'm Lily." I pressed a few keys, ran through a few scales, then nodded. "I'm good. Let's go." I looked and realized the entire room was still staring at me. "What?"

"Let her play," Rafe said.

Oh, lucky me. The leader of the pack gave me the thumbs-up.

I rolled my eyes and started to play from the sheet music in front of me. What did I expect? He was related to Miss Jespersen. Of course he'd be an overbearing, annoying jerkhead who needed to boss everyone around . . . God, this song was awesome!

I was halfway through the first page, dancing and doing a butt wiggle when I realized no one else was playing. My fingers stuttered over the keys. "Am I doing it wrong?" I couldn't take failing twice in the same day. I stepped back from the keyboard, my cheeks suddenly heating up. What had I been thinking, barging in here? I was such an idiot. A little JamieX and I'd lost my mind? "Never mind. Sorry I bothered you. I'll just get my stuff and go—"

"No." Chris held up his hand. "You're awesome."

Warmth flooded through me. "Really?"

"Oh, yeah." He turned to the rest of the group. "Let's go."

Rafe grunted, hit his sticks together in the air for a few counts, then started a strong beat with his drums. The other guitarist joined in, then Angel. Chris pointed at me.

I grinned and started playing.

As soon as Chris started singing, I closed my eyes and let the music wash over me. This was *awesome*. I let my shoulders sway and gave up following the sheet music, letting my fingers flow. Chris's voice was pretty good, sort of

19

melodic and deep, and the rest of the band was decent too. Except Rafe.

Rafe was positively brilliant on the drums, and I let my music follow his. We never looked at each other, but the connection between us was intense and filling the room with such energy that I felt like the walls were going to explode. It was the most amazing feeling I'd ever experienced.

The song ended, and I added an extra little flourish at the end, complete with a full spin, just like in the video. I grinned at the band, who were all high-fiving one another. "That was great," Chris said.

"The best we've ever played it," Angel agreed.

The other guitar player nodded at me. "Nice job, Lily."

I smiled at him. "Sorry I didn't stay on the music, but—"

"No," Angel said. "You did way better than the music we had."

My smile got wider, and I felt like skipping

around the room. "Thanks." I turned to Rafe. "What did you think?"

After a moment he nodded. "You did great."

Goosebumps shot down my arms. I could tell that Rafe didn't say anything nice unless he meant it, and suddenly I felt better than I had in a while.

"Lily!"

The smile dropped from my face and I spun around.

Miss Jespersen was standing in the doorway, her hands on her hips and her face all scrunched up like she'd been sucking on lemons for the last fifty years.

The room fell silent, and I knew I was in deep trouble. "Um . . ."

Rafe started drumming again. "I asked Lily to help us out since Paige is late. Sorry if I screwed up, Aunt Joyce."

I jerked my gaze toward him, stunned by his willingness to face down his aunt in my defense, but he kept his eyes on his aunt.

Miss Jespersen's face tightened. "Your

mother's looking for you, Lily. If you can drag yourself away, I suggest you let her know that you haven't been abducted."

"Yeah, okay." I stepped away from the keyboard, letting my fingers trail over the keys in a farewell moment. Crusty would cut off my fingers before she'd let me waste my time and talent on an electric keyboard. I picked up my backpack and slung it over my shoulder. "So, um, see you guys."

Chris touched my arm. "Can you practice with us again? Like tomorrow?"

"No, she can't." Miss Jespersen flicked his hand off me. "Lily is a gifted musician and doesn't have time for *this* kind of music."

The welcoming expression vanished from Chris's face. Angel seemed surprised and a little offended. The other guitarist shot me a look of pity. I felt my cheeks heat up as I tried to explain: "That's not true, I —"

"*Now*, Lily." Crusty propelled me toward the door and I glanced over my shoulder at Rafe, mouthing the word *thanks*.

He nodded at me just before the door shut behind us.

I couldn't believe he'd actually defended me against his aunt.

So. Totally. Hot.

XOXOX **Chapter Three**

My mom laid a major guilt trip on me for making her and Miss Jespersen think I'd been abducted when I'd bailed from my lesson. I was actually kind of surprised that Miss Jespersen had been worried about me. Almost made her human . . . until she and my mom had lectured me on the audition *again*, brainstorming ways to help me rediscover my passion for piano. Ha! As if! Those days had disappeared the day Miss Jespersen had taken over my life, and I seriously doubted I'd ever see them again.

So by the time school started the next morning, I was more than ready to get out of the house and think about something other than piano. As I rushed into homeroom on Monday, ten minutes early, the only thing keeping me sane was the thought of seeing my friends after two weeks on the road. Sure, it was an all-girls school, but that didn't matter.

"Lily!" My best friend, Erin Reed-Fitzgerald, screamed my name as soon as I got inside the room.

"Erin!" I ran across the room, threw my navy backpack on the floor, and hugged her. "I missed you!"

"Oh, my God, you totally missed out this break." Erin grabbed my arm and tugged me over to where Valerie Collins and Delilah Somers were huddled up. Val and Delilah were the other half of our foursome, though they weren't as tight as Erin and I were. Erin and I had known each other since day care, whereas Val and Delilah had joined our inner circle when we all started attending St. Mary's in the sixth grade. But they were awesome, and I was *so* happy to see them. "Lily's back," she announced.

They screamed and jumped up to hug me, and I screamed back and hugged them. "I'm so psyched to see you guys!" I flopped down next to them at an empty desk. "So, did you guys have a great break, or what?"

"The best," Val said. Her blond hair was blonder than it used to be, and I think she'd gotten even taller. She looked gorgeous, even wearing the navy pants and white shirt of our school dress code.

"But we missed you big-time," Delilah added. Her brown hair had new highlights in it, and she had a tan.

I slid a sideways glance at Erin, who was putting on lip gloss. She had highlights too. Clearly, I'd missed out on a "let's get our hair done" day on the town. Not that I could have participated. Streaked hair was inappropriate for pianists.

"Love the 'do," I said.

Val fluffed her hair. "Thanks! We got it done last week. Came out great, didn't it?"

"Yeah." I fingered my boring dirty-blond

hair and decided I was going to wear a hat tomorrow.

Val held out her cell phone. "So, what do you think of this guy? Cute or not?"

I took the phone and peered at the image of a guy with short blond hair wearing lacrosse pads covered in mud. "Cute."

"See?" Val snatched the phone back. "You have to go to the semiformal with him."

"Me?" I asked. They'd arranged a date for me to *the* biggest event of our freshman year, which was only three weeks away? They were the best friends ever!

"No, you goof. I'm talking about Delilah," Val said. "She's afraid he's not cute enough to be seen with in public." She waggled the phone in Delilah's face. "Lily thinks he's cute."

"He *is* cute." I grabbed the phone from Val and looked at it again. He was way cute. I'd never seen him before. "How'd you meet him?" Since we went to an all-girls school, meeting boys was high on our list of priorities and low on our list of successful activities. Except for Rafe, of course. He was hot, and I'd met him, so life was good. Well, at least not as bad as it had been before he'd defended me to his aunt.

"Delilah met Jeff through me." Val looked smug. "The Inverness lacrosse team was practicing on the next field while I was at softball mini-camp."

Inverness was the boys school across town that was affiliated with our school. Varsity and junior varsity teams from our school used the Inverness fields for practice. I'd never been to Inverness, but I'd dreamed about it. I looked at Val with renewed interest. "You really went to Inverness?"

"Sure did."

"But that's not the best part," Erin interrupted. "Delilah and I went to watch Val's practice and we met this group of guys on the lacrosse team." She grinned. "And they're sophomores."

"Wow. Really?" A glimmer of jealousy flickered through me and my smile got kind of stiff. "I met the governor last week when I—"

"Keith is having a back-to-school pool party on Saturday," Erin interrupted again. "His dad always fills the pool early and heats it, in case of hot weather. And it's supposed to be in the eighties this weekend."

"Keith? Who's Keith?" I asked.

Delilah poked Erin's arm. "You know he's having the party only so he can make a move on you."

Erin's cheeks turned red. "No way! He likes you."

"Nope. Jeff already asked me to the semi," Delilah said.

"No way!" Erin screamed. "When?"

"Last night. And he said Keith wants to ask you, and Hugh's going to ask Val. If you guys go, I'll go."

Val sucked in her breath. "Hugh? Really? He's going to ask me?" She leaned back in the chair. "He's *so* hot."

I tapped Val on the arm. "Who's Hugh? Is he one of the lacrosse players?"

"Hugh's cuter than Jeff." Delilah groaned. "That's so unfair that you get Hugh and I get Jeff."

Who did I get? Anyone? I drummed a pencil

on the desk and tried to get noticed. I cleared my throat extra loudly. "So, are you guys going to fill me in? Who are all these guys?"

They stopped talking and stared at me, like they'd forgotten I was there. It was Erin who recovered first. "Omigosh! You need a date for the semiformal too! You have to come on Saturday. I'm sure Keith could find another friend so there would be four guys there."

"Really? You could get me a date?" My bad mood faded. My first real date? How awesome would that be?

Delilah's head bobbed in agreement. "We definitely could. We'll go to the semi as a four-some."

Val flicked an unseen speck of dirt off her manicured nails. "We should move fast though. The semi's only three weeks away. I bet a lot of the cute guys will be snatched up soon."

"That's okay," Erin said. "Lily will take anyone."

Oooh, I didn't like the sound of *that*. "I'm not going with a loser."

"Well, no, that's not what I meant," Erin said. "It's just that you never meet anyone because you're always practicing, so it's not like you'll find someone on your own."

I frowned. "You guys, I do have a life. I met lots of great people on my tour." Yeah, okay, so none of the Mueller-Fordham students I'd toured with had exactly become my best friends, and none of the guys had been dating material, but it wasn't as if I was a *loser*. Yet. But if I ended up in the NESM secondary school program next year, then they'd be absolutely right. My life would be *over*.

Delilah giggled. "What hot guys did you meet on tour? Some gray-haired mayor of a tiny town in western Mass?"

"Or, I know," Val chimed in. "A geek who plays the violin and drools whenever he has to talk to the opposite sex."

"What about that really skinny guy who plays the flute? He was on tour with you, wasn't he? I'm sure he wouldn't mind leaving the argyle sweater at home for the dance."

Erin giggled. "Can you imagine if you went with him? I love you, but I so wouldn't be able to associate with you in public."

Dismay washed over me. "Howard's not that bad . . ."

Erin sat up. "You guys have to come to Lily's next recital at Mueller-Fordham. You won't believe the geeks who play music. I mean, if you showed them a lacrosse stick, they'd probably run away screaming."

I scowled. "So, you're saying I'm a geek?"

"Not at all." Erin put her arm around me and giggled. "But you're the only non-geek at the place, you have to admit."

I sighed. Except for Rafe, they were right, and I doubted Rafe or anyone in Mass Attack was actually a student there. They probably got Miss Jespersen to arrange cheap practice space since she was Rafe's aunt. "So, I'm cool, then?"

Erin's smile slipped and something like pity flickered in her eyes. "Of course you're cool, but, it's not like you really do much besides play the piano, you know?"

"I do too."

She raised a brow. "What else do you do?"

"I . . ." Crud. I couldn't think of a single thing. "I eat."

"Oh, don't worry," Val said. "We'll get you a date for the dance." She fingered my hair. "Maybe you should get some highlights."

I flipped her hand off, resentment beginning to boil inside me. "I don't need a charity date. I'm—"

"It's okay, Lily," Erin said. "You don't have to pretend with us."

"Pretend what? That I have a life?" The identical expression of pity on all their faces infuriated me. "I can get a date. A hot date. Not a leftover who isn't cute enough for you guys."

"Good." Erin grinned. "Then come to the party on Saturday and pick who you want."

"I will." I sat back in the chair and folded my arms, determined to prove to them I could be as cool as they were. I could jump right into their little clique with their new boys. . . .

Then I remembered I had a recital on

Saturday. Not fair!

Erin sighed at the look on my face. "You can't come, can you? Piano thing?"

"I have to do a recital for a senior citizen banquet thing in Portland, Maine," I muttered.

Val raised her eyebrows, Delilah sighed, and Erin patted my shoulder, shaking her head as Val started to say something.

And that's when I realized how they all saw me. Despite their claims, I was the ugly, loser friend with no life who they took care of because I was too pathetic to take care of myself. Even worse, I was an outsider. While I was gone this vacation, they'd gotten tight. They had the boys, they had the dates, and I was baggage. All because I'd spent the last two weeks on tour instead of hanging out with them.

But they were mistaken. They had to be. For my sake. "You're wrong. I can get a date. A hot guy."

They all looked at me with the same doubtful expression on their faces. "Name one cute guy you know," Erin said.

"Rafe." The name tumbled off my tongue

before I could stop it.

"Rafe? Who's Rafe?" Val looked skeptical. "A guy at the gas station who fills your mom's car?"

"No. He's sixteen, and he's a drummer at Mueller-Fordham. He's way hotter than Jeff."

Delilah wrinkled her nose. "Everyone's hotter than Jeff."

Erin gave me this look, like she felt so bad that I had to lie. "Have you even *met* him?"

"Of course," I said haughtily. "I'm *dating* him."

My three friends stared at me as if I'd gone insane. "You're dating a guy?" Erin asked skeptically. "Your parents would never let you date."

Delilah leaned forward and peered intently at me. "Have you kissed him?"

Uh-oh. If I said I'd kissed him, they'd want a description and Val would know I was lying, because she'd kissed tons of guys. But if I hadn't kissed him, that didn't really count as dating. But I so couldn't take their pity party anymore. Mostly because they were right, and I didn't want them to be.

"Well?" Delilah asked. "Have you?"

I jerked up my shirt and showed them my pale stomach in a most excellent change of subject. "I got a belly-button ring over break."

They gaped at my new jewelry, and Erin slapped her hand over her mouth. "I can't believe it! Did your parents *freak* or what?"

"They don't know." I'd done it with Maria, a flutist who'd been on the tour. We'd snuck out after a particularly miserable recital at this library where there'd been only three people in the audience because it had been a gorgeous Saturday and the rest of the world had been somewhere fun or at least outside. Maria had been the one cool chick on tour, and I think I could have been friends with her, but then she'd gotten invited to solo for some concert series in Europe and she'd left me behind.

But I had the ring; it was a great feeling to be stuck in a boring recital in my frilly dress, knowing I had a belly-button ring that Crusty and my parents would never allow. It hadn't changed my life at all, but it made me feel better. Sometimes. Except when it itched and got caught on things. Washcloths were now banned from my life.

Val touched my gold stud in reverence. "Wow. That is so sweet."

I grinned. "See? I'm not a loser."

Delilah still looked skeptical. "What does Rafe think of it?"

"It was his idea." Well, it probably would be, right? I mean, he seemed like a belly-button-ring kind of guy.

Val sat back in the chair. "It looks good. Did it hurt?"

"Not at all," I lied.

Erin sighed. "I'm so jealous. I thought you were having the worst spring break, and you were off with some boyfriend getting a belly-button ring."

Relief rushed through me at the genuine look of envy on her face. She had no idea as to the truth, and that was the way it would stay, until I could fix my life and actually have something worthwhile to talk about. I dropped my shirt back down as Mrs. Griffith walked into the room and ordered us to our seats.

As I slid into my seat next to Erin, she slipped me a note. *Do you really have a boyfriend?*

I wrote back one word. *Yes!!!!!!*

Are you going to invite him to the semiformal?

Invite Rafe? As if! *He can't come.*

Then who are you going to the semi with?

My mind raced to come up with a believable excuse. I chewed on my pen for a few seconds, then wrote, *I don't think I'll go. It might upset him if I went with someone else.* Yeah, that was why I was going to stay home. Because of my devoted boyfriend. Ha.

Erin snorted and Mrs. Griffith snapped her gaze in our direction. We both huddled over our books and it was a few moments before Erin slid the note back toward me. I checked out Mrs. Griffith, then pulled the note onto my book. *Come with us to Inverness today and pick out a guy. Rafe can get over himself.*

I almost grinned. I had a feeling Rafe *did* need to get over himself. But there was no way I could go to Inverness today. Miss Jespersen would be waiting for me at three o'clock at Mueller-Fordham. With my audition less than three weeks away, I had lessons almost every day. My fingers curled around my textbook at the thought of heading back into that torture chamber.

Erin slid me another note. *So? Are you coming today or what? You have to quadruple date with us to the semi.*

Longing washed over me. If Val, Delilah, and Erin all went to the semi and I stayed home, it would make me even more of an outsider. I so wanted to go. Like, really, really, *really* badly. I drummed my pen on my desk and thought about how I could swing a trip to Inverness this week. My mom worked late on Thursdays and couldn't take me over to Mueller-Fordham. I always took the bus home and practiced on my own.

No one would know if I went to Inverness this Thursday instead, as long as I got home before my mom.

Excitement trilled at the thought of how much trouble I would be in if anyone found out. There was something compelling about the thought of bailing on practice, knowing it was so illegal. *I'll try to make it on Thursday. Okay?*

Erin read my note and gave me the thumbs-up.

God. Did I really have the guts to blow off practice?

I didn't.

Did I?

Chapter Four

XOXOX

At my lesson two days later, Miss Jespersen finally made me cry.

I was sitting there at the stupid piano with the stupid tears trickling down my cheeks, and Crusty's face was all scrunched up in confusion. "Why are you crying?"

Maybe because you just called me a failure for the fiftieth time in the last ten minutes and I can't take it one more second? Yeah, that might be why.

I lifted my chin and sniffled. "I'm not crying. Allergies."

Her eyes narrowed. "Toughen up, Lily.

You'll never be a success if you can't take criticism. You want me to tell you you're great? Well, then, *be* great. I'm not going to prop you up with false praise just to make you feel good. My job is to make you better, and that's what I'm going to do."

I dug my fingernails into my palms and stared at the piano keys. I hated those ugly pieces of ivory. I wished they'd shrivel up into a miserable pile of rabbit poop. How could I ever have enjoyed pounding away at them? It seemed so unreal that I'd actually been the one to beg my parents for lessons in the beginning. Had I known what I was getting into, I would have asked to have my toes amputated without Novocain instead.

"Are you listening to me?" Miss Jespersen said. "Less than two and a half weeks to go, and you're still playing uninspired music."

I gritted my teeth so hard my jaw started to hurt.

"You better stop pouting right now or I'm walking out," she warned.

I'd had it.

"Don't bother." I swung my legs over the piano bench, stood up, then walked out and slammed the door shut behind me.

Miss Jespersen yanked the door open before I'd made it five feet. "Get back in here, Lily!" she commanded. Her voice was low and threatening.

I ignored her and walked down the hallway lined with individual practice rooms. When I walked past an open door that had JamieX pouring out of it, I couldn't stop myself from peeking inside. Rafe was at the drums, and he looked completely cute in a white T-shirt and blue jeans. He saw me at the door, and gave me a nod.

I nodded back, keeping my expression composed. No way was I going to rush in there, throw myself at his feet, and beg him to go to the semiformal with me, though if I thought it might work, I'd consider it.

Chris waved at me in the middle of his singing, and I grinned back.

Angel smiled at me, but the other guitar player ignored me, too into his music to look up.

But what I noticed most was the girl playing the keyboard. She had wild red hair, perfect cheekbones, and she was frowning in concentration.

I was much better than she was.

Miss Jespersen came up behind me and wrapped her fingers around my arm, but I yanked free before she could get a grip. "I'm done," I told her.

"You're finished when I say you're finished," she whispered, like it was some secret threat too horrible to be overheard by Rafe and his friends.

I turned around to face her. "You don't own me."

Her eyes widened in what looked like genuine confusion, but I knew she had to be faking it. "I'm not trying to own you, Lily. I'm trying to help you."

"How? By torturing me? I've had it with how you treat me and I'm so sick of the piano!"

At my words, Crusty's face darkened. I realized the band had stopped playing and everyone was listening.

Involuntarily, I checked out Rafe. He was watching us, but I couldn't read his face at all.

"Lily! Stop flirting with Rafe this instant."

Oh, no. *Tell me she didn't just say that.* Heat flared into my cheeks as Rafe's expression morphed into surprise. He surreptitiously peeked at the keyboard player, who was frowning at me.

Crusty leaned in close. "Get back to the practice room. Now."

I heard Angel snicker. How could Crusty humiliate me like that in front of them? Private torture was one thing, but in front of *them*? It was too much. Unforgivable. "Get away from me," I snapped.

Then I turned and stormed outside.

I stalked out to the front porch of the gorgeous brick house that now housed Mueller-Fordham and sat down on the top step. Over an hour until my mom was due.

I hugged my arms to my chest and dropped my forehead to my knees, preparing for Crusty to come after me. The front door squeaked and I immediately lifted my head and started humming JamieX, wiggling my shoulders with the beat. Yeah, look at me, dancing away because I didn't care about anything.

"You okay?" Rafe asked.

I jerked my gaze up at him. "Yeah. Fine." I *was* fine, now that he was here.

He sat down next to me, so close we almost touched. "That was kinda cool."

I slid a glance at him, but he was watching a sports car drive by. "What was cool? The car?"

His gaze flicked toward me. "No. You telling her off."

"Oh." A feeling of warmth flickered through me. "Oh."

He bumped his shoulder with mine. "Don't take her personally. She's not that bad once you get to know her."

I snorted. "She's been teaching me for three years and I've never seen anything good about her."

He shrugged. "Aunt Joyce can be okay."

Uh-oh. I'd forgotten she was his aunt. I tried to recover. "I'm sure she can be, but I don't bring it out in her. I disappoint her all the time."

"Maybe." He fell silent, and I didn't know what to say, but it didn't feel like an awkward silence. It felt sort of comfortable. "You need a ride?"

I almost choked. "What?"

"A ride. You need one? Paige had to leave early, so we're calling it a night. Angel and Chris hate to practice without a keyboard."

Omigosh. "Yeah, a ride would be great." My heart was racing so fast that my chest actually hurt. "I just need to run inside and call my mom . . ."

He set a phone in my hand, his fingers brushing against my palm. My hand was shaking as I dialed. He had a car *and* a phone *and* was giving me a ride home? I swallowed hard and somehow managed to talk when my mom answered her phone. "Mom, it's me. I got done early with my lesson, so Cru—Miss Jespersen's nephew is giving me a ride home. Is that okay?"

My mom wasn't an idiot. "Why is your lesson over early?"

"Miss Jespersen went insane and had to be carted off in a straitjacket."

"Lily," my mom warned.

I rolled my eyes. "I'll tell you later. Gotta go. Bye." I hung up and handed the phone back to Rafe. His fingers grazed my hand again as he took the phone, and I felt my skin tingle where he'd touched it. I was never going to wash it again. *Ever.*

"Ready?" He stood up and held out his hand to pull me to my feet.

I lifted my hand, and he grabbed it and tugged me up. For like forever, we stood there, like we were holding hands, only a foot apart . . . then he let go, spun around, and jumped down all the steps in one leap. "Let's go, then."

Rafe swung into a black Jeep without a top. "Climb in."

Oh, wow. This was so awesome. I grabbed the roll bar and pulled myself into the passenger seat, plopping down next to him. "Love the car."

"It's a guilt present." He started the engine and put on his seat belt. "Where to?"

I gave him directions as I tugged on my own seat belt, making sure it didn't mess up my scoop-neck white top with the cool embroidery around the collar. I'd picked it out hoping I might run into Rafe. Point for me. "What's a guilt present?"

He pulled out onto the road. "My parents are getting a divorce, so they kicked me out of the house so they could try to kill each other in private. The car was to make them feel better."

"Wow, that's a major bummer. The divorce thing, not the car."

He shrugged. "It is what it is."

"So, where do you live, then? Did they really kick you out?" I couldn't imagine my parents throwing me out. I would *freak out*.

"With my aunt."

I couldn't help the heebie-jeebies from crawling down my spine. "Seriously? You actually live with her?"

"Yep." He eased to a stop at a red light,

rested his forearms on the steering wheel, and turned his head toward me. "What's your story?"

He had dark green eyes, I realized, with long eyelashes that were so cute. "Story about what?" My gaze drifted to his mouth, and his lips. Were they soft? What would it be like if he kissed me? Would he —

"Child prodigy on your good days, piece of dirt on your bad ones," Rafe quoted. "What's up with that?" The light changed and he shifted into first and pulled out.

"I play the piano. My parents and your aunt have high hopes for me, but I'm failing miserably." I chewed my lower lip and watched the trees flash by.

"You seem pretty good to me."

I glanced at him, but he was checking out the rearview mirror, not me. "Maybe you can drop a hint to your aunt over dinner so she'll back off."

"Maybe I will." He turned on his blinker. "Right here?"

"Yep." We fell silent for a while, while I frantically tried to think of something to say that would impress him. All I could come up with was to compliment him on his drumming. Bor-ing. *Think of something scintillating.*

He turned on the radio and started flipping through stations. Great. I was so boring that he was giving up on conversation. Then he grinned and turned it up. "Great song."

It was another JamieX song, an older one that still rocked. "I love this song!" I started singing along immediately.

He flicked me a surprised look. "You're —"

"A terrible singer. I know." I blushed. "Good thing I play an instrument, huh?" I started singing again.

After a second, Rafe started singing too.

I immediately whooped and hit him on the shoulder. "You're awful too!"

He grinned at me, his dimples completely adorable and out of character with his tattoo and scruffy hair. "Good thing I play an instrument, huh?"

I laughed, a warm bubbly feeling exploding through me. "I think you're even worse than I am, and that's nothing to be proud of."

He finally laughed too. He'd been cute when he was doing the über-serious mysterious bad boy thing, but he was beyond gorgeous when he was happy. "You're definitely worse," he said.

"No way. You're insanely jealous of my incredible voice." I turned it up and started singing louder.

He joined in, and we sang the rest of the way to my house. We didn't even stop when we hit the stoplight in the town center, even though there were kids standing on the sidewalk five feet away. They were making fun of us, but we kept singing.

Yeah, those girls were eyeing Rafe. Too bad for them. I was the one making bad music with him, and it rocked!

He pulled into my driveway and turned down the radio. His cheeks were sort of flushed and he was grinning.

"Thanks for the ride, Rafe."

"Anytime, Lily. Despite what my aunt says about you, you're not too bad."

I smacked him lightly on the arm. "Not funny."

His grin faded. "Sorry."

Shoot. I didn't want him to drive off thinking I was some oversensitive loser. "I'm just kidding." I swung out of his Jeep and landed on the driveway with a graceful thump. "If you ever need a stand-in for the keyboard again, let me know."

His smile disappeared and he got this really awkward expression on his face. "Um, about that . . ."

All my happiness suddenly vanished, but I shrugged like I didn't care. "It's no problem. I know you already have a keyboard player. I just meant—"

"She's my girlfriend."

I felt sick. "Who is? Angel?"

"No, Paige. The girl who plays the keyboard."

I took a deep breath and tossed my hair. "Whatever."

"I just didn't want you to think, well, I

mean, because I gave you a ride today and stuff."

Oh, God, this was the worst! I was getting dumped before I'd even dated! "Rafe, seriously, it's no biggie. I was just having fun on the ride home. I have a boyfriend already, so I'm glad it's not an issue," I blurted out before I could stop myself. *Yikes!* Had I really just said that?

Something flickered across his face. "You have a boyfriend?"

Too late to back out now. "Yep. Sophomore over at Inverness. Plays lacrosse." Wow. Two fake boyfriends in three days. My social life was rocking. I managed a smile, even though I felt like running into my house and curling up into a miserable little ball. "He can sing, though, so don't tell him I stink, okay? That's our little secret."

His mouth curved into an intimate smile. "Our little secret," he agreed. "Deal." He started the Jeep back up. "So, I'll see you around."

"If you're lucky."

That same weird look crossed his face again. "If I'm lucky," he repeated. Then he shifted into reverse and backed out of the driveway.

I refused to stand there and stare after him, so I turned and ran into the house, jumping over two geraniums in case he was looking. Girls who had just been rejected by a guy they had a major crush on didn't leap over flowerpots. They sobbed and cried and got all pathetic.

But not me. No way.

I vaulted up the steps, shoved my key in the lock, and danced inside, then slammed the door shut so I could collapse on the floor and be a loser in private.

Chapter Five

I told my mom the truth about what happened at the lesson, and what did she do? She went off to call Miss Jespersen and find out her side, not believing me when I told her that Miss Jespersen was laying the pressure on way too thick.

Lucky for me, Crusty wasn't home, but my mom still made me practice. For *two hours*.

By the end, even my mom admitted I sounded awful. That put me in an even worse mood, especially when she started talking about the audition again.

I practiced for another miserable hour, trying hard to remember what it was like to enjoy piano, but failing miserably.

Then I did homework, because I had nothing else to do.

By Thursday afternoon I was so sick of practicing that I didn't feel even the least bit guilty about playing hooky and sitting on the sidelines at the Inverness practice fields, watching a bunch of guys do drills while Val was at softball practice. Mom was at work. Miss Jespersen was teaching at the school. Everyone trusted sweet little Lily to go home like a good girl and practice.

Not.

I hugged myself, watching the guys. Since when was I the type to cut practice? I wasn't, but I didn't feel like I was doing anything wrong. I felt like I was living! And I was on the verge of discovering the trick to getting myself a *real* boyfriend. I was a rebel!

Erin nudged me. "See number ten? That's Keith. Is he cute or what?"

I studied the field, and got a vague glimpse

of number ten before he disappeared beneath a slew of grunting bodies and lacrosse sticks. "I like his helmet."

Delilah pointed at the pile. "That's Jeff at the bottom." She sighed. "He's not that cute, plus he's getting squashed. I really think I should tell him I can't go to the semiformal with him."

"You *have* to go," Erin said. "He's best friends with Keith and Hugh, and if you don't go, then they might not ask us and then—"

"So, which one's mine?" I was risking the wrath of Miss Jespersen and my parents because my friends had sworn that the guys had a friend who needed a date for the semiformal. I was there to meet him. Since Inverness and St. Mary's hosted the semiformal together, the guys were going to get dates if we didn't snag them first. I had to move in today for the kill, or risk staying home, since my "boyfriend" Rafe was still unable to attend.

And if I got a date, then maybe my friends would forget about Rafe. They hadn't stopped grilling me about him so far, forcing me to make up lies constantly. As of this moment, Rafe and I had been dating for two weeks, had gone to three movies, and he'd given me a stuffed animal. And he was sixteen, birthday in March, and he had written a song about me. Unfortunately, he was not available for the semiformal, but was now okay with me going without him. What a guy.

My plan for the moment was to start to date this Inverness guy, whoever he was, fall in love, and then "break up" with Rafe. Or something like that, so long as it ended with Rafe out of the picture and no one realizing I'd lied about him being my boyfriend.

"I don't know which one's yours," Erin said. "His name's Lesley or something like that."

"Lesley? That's a girl's name." Unlike Rafe. He had a great name.

"Obviously it's not a girl's name," Delilah said. "At least he's got to be cuter than Jeff."

The boys broke out of their huddle around the coach, and suddenly there were three guys jogging toward us clutching their lacrosse sticks. My stomach did a sudden belly flop and my mouth got dry. A boy was on his way over to me. To meet me. To talk to me.

I clutched Erin's arm as she beamed at them. "Hi, Keith." She giggled.

Delilah leaned into my other side as she let out her breath. "Jeff actually looks pretty good with mud on his face," she whispered. "Doesn't he?"

"Yeah, sure." I wet my lips and stared at the boy. Number ten was out, but which of the other two was mine? They both had muddy faces, and they were both pretty cute. Not Rafe, but good enough to be seen with in public.

Then I noticed one of them was looking right at me, and I knew it was *him*. He had light brown hair that was cut short. He smiled at me, and I grinned back, my breath catching in my chest.

He came to a stop in front of me. "You must be Lily."

I nodded. Forgot how to talk.

He flashed me a grin. "I'm Les."

I nodded again, my hands suddenly clammy and my heart racing. What was I supposed to say to him? What did lacrosse players like to talk about? The only guys I talked to were the other students at Mueller-Fordham, and we talked recitals and classical music. No way would Les think that was interesting.

He started walking, and I realized we were all heading back toward the gym. I could handle that. I fell in next to him.

"So, you go to St. Mary's?" he asked.

I nodded. *Think of something interesting to say.* But nothing popped into my head except that I'd just realized that muddy guys were hot. Yeah, not going to say that.

His smile slipped a little. "Do you talk?"

"Of course." *Oh, God.* My voice was totally hoarse. I cleared my throat. "Yeah. Sorry. So, um, you play lacrosse, huh?"

He swung his helmet from his fingertips, and stared at his stick. "Yeah."

Okay, I could talk about that. "Do you score lots of touchdowns?"

He slanted a look at me. "You mean goals?"

Did I? It sounded like I did. "Um, yeah."

His forehead puckered in a little scowl that

would have been adorable if I wasn't completely freaking out right now.

Silence.

Delilah and Erin were up ahead, laughing and flirting with Jeff and Hugh.

Les and I were silent.

Flirt. I should flirt.

How exactly did one flirt? Ah . . .

"So, um, you play a sport?" he asked.

"I play the piano." I immediately relaxed. Piano was something I could talk about for hours. Talking about it with a cute guy suddenly made me forget that I hated it. Anything was good with a hottie walking next to me.

He frowned. "Really? Like classical music?"

"Yep. I spent spring break on tour. I played nursing homes and a couple museum luncheons and at a fund-raiser for clear lakes in southern Maine. And . . ." I trailed off at the glazed look on his face. "And stuff like that."

"Sorry, but I'm not really into the musician thing." He looked pained. "What else do you do?"

Um . . . I chewed my lip and tried to think

of something. Homework and maintaining personal hygiene didn't seem like the best answers.

"Like, have you seen any movies lately?"

"No. I've been pretty busy with the piano. I have this big audition coming up . . ." I trailed off at the grimace on his face. Okay, so he didn't want to hear about the audition. "But I *wanted* to see a movie."

He brightened. "Which one?"

"The one with Matt Damon." Surely Matt Damon was in a movie right now, wasn't he? Maybe.

Les frowned. "He has a movie out right now?"

Or not. Crud. I was *so* bad at this.

He began to twirl his lacrosse stick, a little desperately. "What about television? What's your favorite show?"

I grimaced as my heart began to pound. "I don't really get to watch much TV."

"Because you're playing the piano."

"Yeah." But I wasn't a loser! There had to be something interesting about me, didn't there? Like . . . um . . .

He grunted. "You watch sports?"

"Not a lot, but, um, I'd really like to learn about lacrosse."

Interest flickered on his face. "Really? You want to come watch my game on Friday night?"

I grimaced again. "I'd really like to, but I can't."

"Piano?"

God, the look of pity he gave me was totally embarrassing. "No, I'm going to rob a convenience store. Want to come?"

He stared at me.

"I'm kidding." I gave a weak laugh. "Joke." In my head, it had sounded better than admitting I was tied up with piano, but it hadn't come out so well. Obviously, Inverness guys didn't think jokes about robbing convenience stores were funny. Rafe would probably think it was hilarious. Too bad Rafe had a girlfriend who was terrible at the keyboard.

"Yeah, well, I gotta go change. It was good to meet you." Les took off in a sprint, ditching me in the middle of the fields.

He was running away. From me. Both my fake boyfriends had ditched me before anything had even started. That had to be a record of some kind.

I saw Erin glance back at me as Les ran past her, and she raised her eyebrows and gave me a thumbs-up.

I managed to grin and nod.

What were the chances Les was going to go to the semiformal with me?

Zero.

I was so hosed.

Chapter Six

Three hours later, I slammed my forehead into the piano keys with a horrendous clang and screamed. Why couldn't I play anymore? I had trophies all over the house, but every time I touched the keys, my playing got worse, like some horrible nightmare I couldn't wake up from. What was *wrong* with me?

I couldn't play the piano, and I'd been shot down by two fake boyfriends. There was nothing redeemable at all. Not even my belly-button ring.

I banged my head on the keys again, the

crash of the chords a horrible noise of misery. Maybe I should start playing with my head. It sounded better than when I used my hands.

The phone rang and I jerked upright. *Please let that be Rafe calling to tell me he dumped his girlfriend because he's so hopelessly in love with me!*

My mom answered the phone. "Well, hello, Erin. I'm sorry, but she's still practicing. Can she call you later?"

"Wait!" I jumped up and ran into the kitchen, where my mom was making dinner. "I need to talk to her."

Mom gave me her "mom" look. "Have you finished practicing?"

"It's about homework."

She raised her eyebrows.

"I'm serious, Mom. It'll take two minutes."

She sighed. "Miss Jespersen said you need to focus. The audition is soon and you aren't nearly sharp enough."

I gritted my teeth against the urge to close my eyes and scream until my brain exploded. "Two minutes."

She held out the phone. "I'll time you."

"Thanks!" I grabbed the phone and took it back into the family room. "Erin? What's up?"

"You have to come to the party on Saturday."

"I want to." I sighed and closed the door. "But I can't. There's no way I can swing that. I have this recital and—"

"No, you *have* to," Erin interrupted. "Les thought you were cute."

"No way!" My breath caught and I immediately felt a million times better. "He did? Seriously? You aren't lying, are you?"

"*But* he thought you were a little weird and possibly lacking in personality."

I sank onto the piano bench, clutching the phone in dismay. "Really? Are you sure?"

"I don't know what you said to him, but if you don't come to the party and redeem yourself, I doubt he'll go to the semiformal with you."

Anxiety rippled over me. "Redeem myself? How?"

"Be funny. Talk about something besides

the piano. Flirt."

I bit my lip and fought against the rising panic. I didn't have a personality, not like my friends did. I was who I was. How was I supposed to fake a life I didn't have? "Maybe it's not a good idea. Rafe called tonight and said he wasn't that high on me going with Les." Fake boyfriend to the rescue. Sigh.

Erin snorted. "So what? If Rafe won't go with you, it's too bad for him. You have to go. It's *the* event of the year! Don't you know that this is the dance where we establish the group of guys we're going to hang out with for the rest of our high school career? If we don't get in with these guys, we're going to spend the next three and a half years spending our Friday nights doing homework." She sighed. "You *have* to be part of the group, Lily. It would be horrible without you. Please?"

Oh, man. I wanted to go so badly. "Erin—"

She groaned. "My mom's yelling at me to clean my room. I have to go. I'll talk to you at school tomorrow. Party's at two on Saturday.

Please find a way to be there, okay? Gotta go. Bye."

She hung up and I threw the phone at the couch. It bounced off and then hit the floor with a crash. The battery cover flew off and ricocheted under the coffee table and the phone beeped, then died. This was so unfair!

My mom opened the door and stuck her head inside. "Time's up. Practice."

I took a deep breath. "Mom, I really need to do some studying with Erin on Saturday for this project we have. Can I go over to her house for a few hours in the afternoon?"

My mom's eyebrows went up. "You have a recital."

I clenched my fists. "I want to skip it."

Her brows went even higher. "You can't skip a recital. What's wrong with you?"

I spun around so I was facing her. "One day off. That's all I want. Why is that so much to ask?"

"Because your audition is two weeks from

Saturday. Miss Jespersen said you need practice."

"But what if I don't want to do it?"

My mom frowned. "Do what? The audition?"

"Piano."

A dark silence fell over the room. "Is Erin trying to talk you out of playing the piano? Because if she is, I don't want you spending time with her."

"No, it's not Erin. It's me. Why can't I—"

The doorbell rang, and a relieved look washed over my mom's face. "I'll get that."

She disappeared, no doubt planning to call Miss Jespersen to find out how to deal with me as soon as she got rid of whoever was at the door. I didn't know who was pushing me harder, my mom or Miss Jespersen. Together, they were too much.

I groaned and flopped back on the piano bench, my head hitting the wood with a thud as I lay down. "Ow." I propped my feet up on the piano in a show of total disrespect for the instrument and stared at the ceiling, thinking about the party, trying to figure out how in the world I could get there.

"Lily."

I didn't even look at my mom. "Who was at the door?"

"Miss Jespersen."

I made a face. "Did she drop off a list of ways to torture me?"

"No, I didn't," my piano teacher said.

Yikes. I scrambled to my feet, wishing that for *once* I could manage to keep from making a total idiot of myself. Crusty stood next to my mom in the doorway, and even my *dad* was there, standing behind them. All of them looked way serious, and I felt a shimmer of panic crawl up my spine. Even thinking of her as Rafe's aunt didn't keep me from wanting to jump through the window and run away screaming.

I swallowed hard and lifted my chin. "What's up?"

Chapter Seven

My parents and Miss Jespersen filed into the family room and lined up on the couch.

I sat on the piano bench, twitching while I waited for them to attack.

"Where were you after school today?" my dad asked.

I felt the blood drain from my face. How did they know I'd bailed on practicing?

"I came by at three thirty to drop off the backpack you left behind yesterday," Miss Jespersen said. "You weren't here. I was so worried that I had to come back tonight and make sure everything was all right."

Oh, no. I was so busted!

My mom eyed me. "Not only are we concerned that you obviously lied to us about where you were, but the bigger concern is this audition. You can't afford to take a day off from practice right now."

Crusty nodded, her eyes beady and demanding as usual, but when I saw the look of annoyance on my dad's face, it was too much.

"Stop it!" I jumped to my feet. "I'm sick of this!"

"Lily, sit down," my mom said. "Now."

But my dad set his hand on her leg and looked at me. "Sick of what, Lil?"

"Piano. Being tortured. Having no friends and no life." I glared at my mom and Miss Jespersen. "Being told I'm a failure fifty times a lesson. I'm not a loser and I'm sick of you trying to convince me I am!"

"Of course you're not a loser, or a failure," my dad said. "Why would you think that?"

I pointed at Crusty. "Because she tells me that all the time."

My parents looked at Miss Jespersen and her sweet old lady look vanished.

"And Mom backs her up," I added.

It was my mom's turn to look shocked, and I felt better immediately.

"Lily, I'm merely trying to push you to be the great pianist I know you can be," Miss Jespersen said. "I wouldn't be doing you any favors if I complimented you when—"

I covered my ears and scrunched my eyes closed. "Shut up! Just stop it! I can't take it anymore!"

"Lily!" My mom looked horrified. "Apologize to Miss Jespersen immediately!"

"No! I used to be good, okay? But I'm not anymore. I stink at the piano. I'm never going to live up to my potential, even if I practice until my fingers turn into bloody stumps! I can't take all this pressure, and I'm tired of not being able to have a life! I hate it!" Tears were streaming down my cheeks, but I didn't care.

Let them see what they were doing to me.

My dad narrowed his eyes thoughtfully, while my mom went crazy, telling me I didn't appreciate the opportunities I'd been given, and Crusty started talking about getting me counseling to handle the stress of being a child prodigy. My chest heaving with sobs, I stared at my dad, both of us ignoring my mom and Crusty. My dad didn't usually get involved in the piano stuff. It was my mom and Miss Jespersen's deal.

"Do you want to quit the piano?" he asked me.

My mom and Crusty shut up when I nodded.

"Are you sure?" he asked.

"Yes." Was he really going to let me do it? Could I really become normal? My throat tightened at the thought of not having any more pressure, of never facing the threat of failure again. Oh, God. Was it really over?

"No," my mom whispered. "She can't quit."

Miss Jespersen said nothing, but she was

looking at me with the strangest look on her face, like she'd never seen me before.

"Why didn't you mention this sooner?" my dad asked.

"I did! I tell Mom all the time."

We both looked at her, and her face paled. "But this is your dream," she said. "I'm just trying to support it."

"No, Mom. It's *your* dream."

"Lily!" My mom looked ill. "What are you saying? You love the piano!"

"I used to. I hate it now." I couldn't keep the bitterness out of my voice.

"Lily, go upstairs," my dad said quietly. "We need to discuss this."

Grateful for the reprieve, I nodded and bolted for the door.

Erin and I spent the next tortured hour on the phone trying to predict the outcome of the Summit Meeting, while we waited for my sentencing.

Finally someone knocked on my door.

I jerked upright. "They're here," I whispered.

"You *have* to call me back as soon as they're gone," Erin ordered. "No matter what time. Swear?"

The doorknob turned. "Lily? Are you still up?"

"I swear." I hung up and shoved the phone under my pillow, then hugged my arms to my chest as my mom and dad walked in the room. When I saw there was no piano teacher lurking behind them, I sighed with relief.

"You okay, Lil?" my dad asked.

"Fine." I eyed them as they sat down on my bed, one on each side, like they were trying to block my path to the exit. "What's up?"

My mom folded her arms over her chest and pursed her lips at my dad. "Hank? You tell her."

Oh, I knew that look. My mom so wasn't happy with the decision. *Please let that mean that I'm free.*

But I could tell by the smile my dad gave

me that I wasn't getting my way. "We'll make a deal with you."

A deal? That had potential. "What kind of deal?"

"You can stop taking lessons with Miss Jespersen."

My eyes immediately filled up with tears. "Really? You promise?"

"Is she really that bad?" My mom sounded so sad that I couldn't tell her the truth.

So I said nothing. I mean, I wasn't going to lie, either.

"But," my dad continued, "we all agree your talent is too much to give up on."

I gritted my teeth and felt all the pressure crush back down on my shoulders.

"However, we also agree that you've lost your passion for music."

Amen to that.

"Miss Jespersen said she saw the old you when you were playing with her nephew's band," my dad said.

I jerked my gaze to his face. "So?"

"So . . . for one month, you can skip your piano lessons and regular practice, as long as you practice with Rafe's band. Apparently, it's a bunch of kids from his high school who get together and occasionally do concerts for free. No pressure. Just fun music."

My mom leaned forward. "Miss Jespersen believes it will help you find your passion again."

"But . . ." Sentenced to playing with Mass Attack? That was great news, not punishment. I swear, sometimes parents are completely insane, not that I was complaining. "But they already have a keyboard player."

"Miss Jespersen assures us it won't be a problem. Rafe's going to call you tonight with the practice schedule." My dad tapped my foot with his finger. "If you skip out on the band even once, it's back to piano with Crusty again. Got it?" My mom cleared her throat and my dad grimaced. "I mean, Miss Jespersen. You shouldn't call her Crusty. It's disrespectful."

I grinned, suddenly unable to contain myself. I was going to get to play with Mass

Attack! I'd impress Rafe with my amazing keyboard talents, he'd fall in love with me, and everyone would think I was cool because I was in a band *and* dating a hot drummer. My life would be perfect. "I agree to the deal."

"There's one more thing," my dad added.

"Anything!"

He smiled at my energy. "It's good to see you happy about music again, hon." He patted my mom's hand. "Isn't it?"

She nodded, but her mouth was tight. It was her guilt look, but I wasn't going to feel bad about it.

"The rest of the deal is that as long as you keep playing with Rafe's band, we'll let you postpone the audition until fall semester, so you'd start NESM in the winter term."

Relief swept over me. "Really? That would be awesome."

My mom sighed. "You really don't want to go to NESM?"

"I can't take it, Mom. Not right now." Just the thought of not having it forced on me in two weeks made me feel better.

Mom started to protest, but my dad squeezed her hand. "You said you trust Miss Jespersen, Mary. Let's give this a try."

No way! This had been Miss Jespersen's idea? Having me play with Rafe's band and postponing the audition? She'd come through for me? Maybe Rafe was right that his aunt wasn't all bad. *Maybe*. I wasn't ready to concede at this point, but for her to talk my mom out of daily lessons . . . wow. She and my dad must have seriously pressured her.

The phone rang, and my heart nearly jumped out of my body. Was that Rafe calling me? How should I react? Should I be surprised? Should I—

My mom raised her brows at the muffled sound of the phone, then reached under my pillow and pulled it out. "Hello?"

She sighed and held the phone out to me. "It's Rafe."

My heart raced. What should I say? Should I sing off-tune again to remind him of our bonding session?

My mom waggled the receiver in my face. "Lily?"

I took the phone and clutched it to my chest. "Can I have some privacy?"

"Sure." My mom trailed her hand through my hair, then let my dad tug her out of the room.

The door clicked shut and I took a deep breath. Rafe *got* music. *He'd* think I was interesting, wouldn't he? We had something in common. We were going to be in a *band* together. How *awesome*. I checked my hair in the mirror, put on some lip gloss, then sat on my pink comforter and crossed my legs. I took a deep breath, then put the phone to my ear. "Hello?" My voice barely shook at all. I was so in control.

"Lily?" His deep voice rumbled across the phone line and I curled my toes into the bedspread.

"Yeah, it's me. My parents just came in here and told me that I'm in your band for the next month. Cool, huh?"

"I don't know what stunt you pulled to get my aunt to come in here tonight and order me to dump my own girlfriend from the band, but it's total crap. What's *wrong* with you?"

The elation whooshed out of me. "It wasn't my idea at all! I told them I wanted to quit piano and then they came up here and told me and—"

"I don't care. Paige is furious with me. You think you're special because you go to St. Mary's and have this perfect little life and everyone tells you you're this child prodigy? Well, forget it. You have no right to screw up my life just so you can have the world adore you."

"Rafe!" I jumped to my feet. "Shut up!"

There was a long silence. "You have *no* right to tell me to shut up."

"*You* have no right to accuse me of any of this! You think I want to hang out with you all day? Forget it! My boyfriend's going to be completely ticked off too, so I'm in the same boat!" I wasn't going to feel bad about that lie.

He deserved it. "So back off! I wanted to quit piano, not be stuck practicing with a dumb band!"

There was a sharp intake of breath on his end. "My band's not dumb."

I relented a little. "Well, maybe your band isn't, but you're being a jerk."

"*I'm* a jerk?"

"Yes. You're accusing me of things I didn't do, and you're not even giving me a chance to explain."

"No explanation needed. Paige and my band were the only good things in my life and you managed to screw them *both* up."

"Fine! I'll go find my parents and tell them I won't do it!"

"It won't matter! My aunt has decided this is what needs to be done to save your precious career, and she won't back off, no matter what you do. Your career in exchange for my life." The hostility in his tone told me exactly what he thought of that trade.

Suddenly, I had a realization that made a

new knot tighten at the back of my throat. "This is all a test, isn't it?"

He paused. "What are you talking about?"

"A test. To see if I really am the failure they think I am." I closed my eyes and sank back on my pillows. The band had been fun that one day because I did it myself. Doing it because Rafe's aunt was trying to save my career would be no different than piano lessons. This was simply more pressure, one more way to fail. I pressed my hand to my forehead. "Forget it, Rafe. I'm not going to do it." I felt sick again. "Tell Paige she's in."

Rafe was quiet for a moment. "You're serious?"

"Yeah."

He sighed. "Lily, you can't quit now."

"No, I'm going to." I sat up, rolled my feet to the floor, and stalked across the room to the door. "I'm just going to tell them piano is over for me, all the way. No band or anything. They can't force me."

"Forget it, Lily. It's too late for that."

I yanked the door open. "No, it's not." I

raised my voice. "Mom? Dad? Where are you?"

"Downstairs," my mom yelled back, and I started to run down the stairs, my heart thudding with the enormity of what I was going to do.

"Lily! Wait!" Rafe said.

I jumped over the bottom step. "What, Rafe? I have to go." I walked into the living room, where my parents were huddled on the couch in deep conversation. They both looked up when I walked in and stopped talking.

Rafe grunted with annoyance. "My aunt will be all over me if you refuse to do it. She'll blame me, and make my life miserable." A noise that sounded like a crash came from his end.

I thought about what he'd said. If I played in the band, he'd hate me for messing up Mass Attack and Paige for a month; but if I didn't, I'd screw up the band forever. I sighed. Like I wanted to deal with his attitude for a month . . . but how could I leave him to his aunt's mercy? I couldn't abandon a fellow victim, especially since this was my fault anyway. But I didn't want to play just to make Crusty happy. I didn't want the pressure anymore. I couldn't take the stress. "Is your aunt planning to attend rehearsals?"

He made a snort of protest. "God, I hope not."

"Hang on." I took the phone away from my mouth and addressed my parents. "Is Miss Jespersen planning to come to rehearsals?"

My mom glanced at my dad. "I think she's planning to stop by, hon. Not to coach you, just to check in."

Rafe overheard her comment. "No way," he protested. "That's so wrong!"

"Forget it, Mom." I folded my arms over my chest. "I'm not playing in the band if she's going to be there. Either I do this band thing on my own and none of you are allowed to interfere, or I'm quitting piano entirely." It was the only solution I could think of that ended up with Rafe not hating me forever and me not losing my mind. I focused my gaze on my dad, because he was the only one who might go against Miss Jespersen.

Dad nodded. "Fine." He put his hand on my mom's arm before she could refuse. "She needs this. Let her do it."

My mom looked at me. "You better be on that keyboard. Sitting in the same room and just watching doesn't count."

I rolled my eyes. "Fine." I turned and walked out, putting the phone next to my mouth again. "Happy, Rafe?"

"You almost blew it," Rafe said. "Are you insane? Didn't you hear me tell you that if you dropped out my aunt would never let me forget it?"

I grinned at how stressed he sounded. *Welcome to my world.* "I'll play on one condition."

He groaned. "What condition?"

"You won't be a jerk to me the whole time."

"Fine. I'll be a jerk only some of the time."

"Rafe!"

He coughed to cover his laughter. Jerk. "Six o'clock tomorrow at Mueller-Fordham. Plan to stay late. We have a gig a week from Saturday and you have a lot of music to learn."

I tripped on the stairs. "A *what*?"

"Gig. We're booked to play a middle school dance. See ya."

I stared at the phone. A gig? Like a piano recital in disguise, only this time I'd have Rafe glaring at me instead of my piano teacher looming over me.

He so owed me for doing this.

Chapter Eight

XOXOX

At five minutes before six on Friday, Erin's mom pulled up in front of Mueller-Fordham to drop me off for band practice. She'd taken the four of us to the mall to shop for new bikinis for the pool party on Saturday, which I was now attending since I didn't have a recital.

I'd never worn a bikini before. It was black. Completely sexy. I felt naked with it on and there was *no way* I was going to wear it at the pool party in front of *boys*.

But I'd bought it anyway.

Had to. Like I wasn't going to buy it when Val, Delilah, and Erin had all bought bikinis.

I'd been pumped to spend the afternoon with my friends, but it had been miserable. Nothing like discovering you're the only one still wearing a stretchy white junior bra to make you feel like a dork. My friends had all gone to Victoria's Secret over spring break and bought real bras.

Nice of them to tell me before I'd yanked off my shirt in the dressing room and they all started cracking up. Even my belly-button ring hadn't been enough to save me. Now, for the first time in ages, I was actually looking forward to getting out of the car and into the music school.

Of course, that might have had something to do with the fact I was about to go play with Rafe's band.

"Can we come in with you?" Val asked. "I want to meet Rafe."

"No." I hugged my shopping bag to my chest as I recalled that Rafe was still mad at me. After my humiliation this afternoon, I was so not up for dealing with Rafe's hostility. Wasn't the first day of my Crusty-free existence supposed to be perfect?

"Why not?" Val nudged me. "Does Rafe even exist? Who wants to bet that Lily's going to her piano lesson, same as usual today?"

Erin's mom looked back at us. "Val. Knock it off."

I grinned, and she winked at me. I love Erin's mom. She's way cooler than mine.

Delilah opened the door and got out. "I agree with Val. I don't think Rafe exists. If Lily was really dating some hottie, she wouldn't still be wearing junior bras."

I scrambled out and grabbed her wrist as she started walking into the music school. "Hey! Don't go in."

Val was on the sidewalk next to me. "'Fess up, Lily. You've been lying to us since we got back from spring break."

"Get back in the car, girls," Erin's mom said, even as Erin climbed out of the car.

Erin stood next to me. "I believe her."

Relief washed over me, and I smiled at Erin.

"And she'll take us in there and prove it, and then you two will look like fools," she finished.

Oh, *thanks*.

She tucked her arm through mine and beamed at me. "Let's go, Lily."

Before I could come up with an excuse, a certain black Jeep pulled into the parking lot. *Rafe.* He was wearing sunglasses, a denim jacket, and his hair was all messed up from the wind. So hot.

Val sucked in her breath as he swung down from the Jeep. "Who is *he*?"

Please don't let him notice me. If he came over and yelled at me for wrecking his relationship with his actual girlfriend, my life would be over. Forever.

"Complete hottie," Erin agreed. "I'm in love."

"Me too." Delilah ran her fingers through her hair. "Do I look okay?"

Then he looked over. Of course he would. Four girls standing on the street right in front of the school. Like he wouldn't notice. He scanned the group, and I felt my cheeks heat up as his gaze landed on me. His mouth tightened ever so slightly, and I knew he was still mad.

I had to bail before he got to us. But where? And if I bailed, everyone would know I was lying.

There was only one option. If it didn't work, I was so dead.

I yanked my arm out of Erin's and ran across the lawn toward Rafe to intercept him before he could get within earshot of my friends. His eyes widened when he saw me running toward him, and he raised his arms like he was going to fend me off.

I launched myself at him. My body slammed into his with a thud and I threw my arms around his neck. "Rafe!" I said it loud enough for my friends to hear.

He grunted from the impact and grabbed me around the waist to keep me from knocking us both over, and my heart thudded down to my toes. This was what a real hug with a guy was like? No wonder Val did it all the time! *Wow!*

He set me back down, his hands still on my hips. His face was wary and he looked like he was afraid I'd gone insane. "What was that about?"

I knew my friends couldn't hear us, as long as we talked quietly. I wrapped my hands around his arms, like I was using him for balance, and tried not to think about the fact I could feel his muscles. "I wanted to apologize for getting you sucked into my miserable life. Your life is bad enough already, and I'm sorry." I hadn't meant to apologize, but suddenly, it seemed like the right thing to do. Not that I was one of those girls who'd give up their personality for a cute guy, though. "But you were still a jerk for how you treated me last night."

The corner of his mouth curved up and he let go of my waist to brush my bangs off my face. When my dad did that, I felt like he was treating me like a little kid. When Rafe did it, I felt like my legs were going to melt and I was going to die right there.

"Sorry about last night," he said.

I blinked and this time had to hold on to him for real to keep from falling over. "What?"

He shrugged. "I talked to my aunt afterward. She said you had nothing to do with it."

"I didn't."

He raised a brow. "I know. I just said that."

Jerk. Like he had to point out that I was a total idiot when I was around him? "So, what's your point?"

"The point is, I'm sorry. I was a jerk and you didn't deserve it."

"Oh." Well, that was kind of nice. Did I still have to be mad at him?

He gave my ponytail a tug. "So, what do you say to a truce? We're stuck with each other for a month, right? We might as well deal with it."

I grinned. "I suppose I can forgive you. But only because you're a good drummer, not because you deserve it."

He chuckled. "Such attitude. How does your boyfriend stand it?"

Oh, right. I forgot about my boyfriend. He had a girlfriend. I had a boyfriend. The ponytail tugging meant nothing. "My boyfriend thinks I'm a goddess. He's right, of course."

His smile got wider. "You'd be impossible as a girlfriend, you know that?"

My smile faltered. Then I slapped on my most arrogant look, the one I used when I was feeling the most scared at a recital and didn't want to show it. "You're just jealous." I spun away with a flip of my hair and started marching toward the building.

I peeked at my friends as Rafe caught up and opened the door for me. They were all staring at us with their mouths hanging open in shock.

The look of stunned disbelief was almost enough to make up for the fact that Rafe thought I would be a terrible girlfriend.

Almost, but not quite.

I walked into the band room a few minutes later, and Chris nodded at me. "Good to have you back, Lily."

I immediately relaxed under his warmth and

smiled back. "I was tortured into it."

"So I heard." He was wearing a pair of black jeans and a plain black T-shirt. His blond hair was sort of wavy, and I realized he had really blue eyes. How could I not have noticed them before?

A heavy hand landed on my shoulder and I looked up to find Rafe standing next to me, frowning. "You haven't met our bass player. Lily, this is Nash. Nash, Lily."

Nash was tuning his guitar, but he looked up and gave me a nod. I nodded back, and then he returned to his instrument.

"Nash doesn't say much," Rafe said. He tightened his grip on my shoulder and turned me away from Chris and steered me toward the keyboard in the corner. "But he knows a lot. If I'm not here, he's the one you should go to with questions."

Chris snorted and I glanced at him. He winked at me. "I'm the expert."

"I have no doubt," I replied, then grinned when Rafe's scowl got even deeper. I elbowed him. "Lighten up, Rafe. We're just messing with you."

"We're here to play, not socialize."

Chris rolled his eyes and Angel snorted. "You'd never guess he used to be fun, would you?"

Rafe glared at Angel. "Stuff it, Angel."

"Or what? You stopped having any input over me when we stopped dating."

I knew it! There had been an undercurrent of something between them that first day. That meant that Rafe not only had a current girlfriend in his band, but also a gorgeous ex-girlfriend. I was completely outnumbered.

Rafe squeezed my shoulder. "Ignore her."

I slanted a look at him, ready to give him attitude for trying to tell me what to do, but I clamped my lips shut at the look of pain in his eyes. He was upset by what Angel had said! Why? Because she'd pointed out that they were no longer dating? Or because she said he used to be fun?

Rafe bent over the keyboard, hiding his face from me as his fingers flew over the keys.

"That's the melody I want you to play. Got it?" He looked up when I didn't answer him. "What?"

How could I answer him? I was too shocked.

He finally grinned. "I play the keyboard a little."

"And the guitar," Angel complained. "That's why he thinks he's in charge of the band, because he can do everything."

I met his gaze. "Except sing," I whispered.

His eyes sparkled and he touched his index finger to my lips, before turning away. "Okay, guys, let's get going. I have to hit the road early tonight."

Angel raised her eyebrows. "Early? Since when do you cut out early? It's Friday night. Shouldn't we be here until midnight?"

Midnight? He was worse than Crusty.

Rafe sat down at his drums. "Gotta take Paige out. She's a little testy today."

I made a point of leafing through the sheet music. It wasn't my fault and I wasn't going to feel bad about Paige. Yeah, that's why my stomach hurt at the mention of his girlfriend. Guilt.

Not jealousy or anything stupid like *that*.

We started off with a new song, the one Rafe had shown me the melody for. I messed up the first time. "Sorry." I didn't look up and I tried it once more, screwing up the notes again. *"Sorry."* Oh, God. I was a failure already.

"Hey, Lily."

I looked up at Rafe. "What?" He was going to kick me out, wasn't he?

"You're doing great."

I shook my head. "No, I'm terrible. I know I'm messing you guys up, and I promise I'll get it. I'm trying, I really am."

"Chill out, Lily," Chris said.

I looked up at the easy tone in his voice. He didn't sound mad.

"It took Paige a month to even figure out what key it was in," Chris said. "Trust me, you're already way ahead of where she ever was."

I shook my head and frantically pushed my hair out of my eyes. "It doesn't matter. I'm better than this. I'm letting you guys down and—"

"Okay, gang, we're switching songs," Rafe

interrupted. "The new JamieX song. Everyone on board?"

I almost cried with relief. I knew I could do that one. I didn't need music for it. I gave Rafe a look of thanks, and he winked at me.

Rafe hit the drum intro to the song and I felt the beat inch into my gut, past my embarrassment. I lifted my head as Nash and Angel started in and I felt the song roll over me.

Chris nodded in time.

I took a deep breath and started playing the notes dotted across the sheet music. Nice and precise. Get all the notes right. I could do it without mistakes.

Then Rafe veered off the sheet music and started challenging me the same way he had the last time we'd played together. I shook my head at him. I couldn't do that right now. I had to concentrate.

He kept playing. Challenge flashed in his eyes, and I finally stuck my tongue out at him.

He grinned and amped it up even more.

Fine. Be that way. I ditched the sheet music and started improvising with him.

The rest of the group stopped playing, as Rafe and I played harder, throwing ourselves into the music. I closed my eyes and let the song invade my body, let my heart crash in rhythm with Rafe's drums. We plowed through the song without stopping, ending in a battle between Rafe and me that shook the walls. He ended with a brilliant drum solo and then threw his sticks up in the air with a whoop, catching them perfectly.

I leaned back on my heels and laughed out loud, adrenaline rushing through me.

"If you two are done showing off, we could try that again as an actual band," Chris remarked dryly.

"Or you guys could try to keep up," Rafe shot back.

"Or we could throw you out the window," Chris said.

Angel grinned at me and rolled her eyes. I returned the smile.

This was *way* better than piano lessons.

After Rafe and Chris finished knocking each other around, we started to practice seriously.

We'd been working on JamieX for almost an hour and I was having a total blast when Miss Jespersen stuck her head in the room.

My fingers immediately stumbled over the keys. Rafe shot me a questioning look, then he followed my gaze to the door and frowned. Crusty walked into the room and sat down in the corner, folding her arms over her chest. I messed up and she made a grunt of disapproval. My throat tightened up and my fingers stiffened.

No! I would not let her ruin this for me! I jerked my eyes away from her and concentrated on the music, and then screwed up *again*.

"I need a break," Rafe said suddenly. He tossed his drumsticks on the floor. "Lily. Come with me."

I clenched my fists and tried to calm down. Why did I let her get to me like this? So what if her disapproval was so thick I could barely breathe? What right did she have to judge me?

Rafe suddenly appeared behind me, his chest brushing against my back. "Lily." His voice was quiet, for my ears only. "Come on." He wrapped his fingers around my wrist and tugged my hand. "I have soda in my car," he said to the rest of the band. "We'll be right back."

Angel raised her brows at me, but I was too upset to worry about it. I let Rafe pull me out of the room, right past Crusty and her prunish face and out into the parking lot.

Chapter Nine

XOXOX

Rafe didn't let go of me until we got to the car, and I didn't try to pull away. We were both dating other people (ahem) so it didn't mean anything, but I still felt better with him touching me. So sue me. It wasn't like I was trying to break up his relationship or anything.

He dropped my wrist and reached into the back of the Jeep. "I'll talk to my aunt and ask her not to come to any more rehearsals. Don't let her get to you."

There was no point in lying. He knew what

was up with me. "How can I not?"

He retrieved a paper grocery bag and set it in my arms. "She likes you, Lily. That's why she's here. She's just trying to support you."

"No, she's trying to pressure me! Do you have any idea what it's like to be called a failure all the time?" I blinked at the sudden moisture in my eyes. What was *wrong* with me these days? I hated crying! "She has no right to make me feel so bad!"

He brushed his fingers over my cheek, and I froze. "You don't suck, Lily."

I swallowed hard. The bag was heavy, so I hugged it to my chest. "That's not what she says."

"So? Who cares what adults say? You think they're always right?" He turned away, his hand dropping from my face.

I bit my lip while he fished another bag out of the Jeep. "You don't think she's right?"

He hoisted the bag onto his hip. "Adults have their own baggage and they take it out on us. The only thing to do is blow them off."

A smile pulled at the corner of my mouth at his flippant attitude. Like it was that easy. "How am I supposed to blow her off? She's in there giving me the evil eye."

"So what? Doesn't mean you have to let it bug you."

I raised my eyebrows. "If you're so tough, how come she was able to bully you into letting me in the band?"

He shrugged. "I decided it was easier to go along with her than fight it, which is not the same thing as allowing her to ruin my life. Besides, I owe her. She got us free practice space at the school." His eyes narrowed and he averted his gaze from me. "Plus, I gotta keep her happy enough so she doesn't ditch me. Next step foster care, right?"

I couldn't stop my mouth from dropping open. "Seriously? Your parents would let you go to foster care?"

He turned away and started walking back toward the building. "Let's go."

"Hey!" I tried to catch up to him, but there

was no way I could run with my bag of drinks. So I sort of hobbled across the lawn. "I didn't mean to offend you. . . ."

"You got plans for Sunday morning?"

I blinked at the change in subject. "Um, I usually practice the piano then, so I guess I'm free."

"Meet me here at nine. I'll get you up to speed on the new material."

I wrinkled my nose at his back. "You're more of a slave driver than Crusty is."

"Or you can learn it in front of the band," he said.

Ah, no thanks. "Fine. I'll see if my mom can drive me."

"I'll pick you up. It's on my way."

Yes! I should have Erin spend the night so she can see him pick me up. "I guess that would be okay."

"Good." He stopped to let me catch up. As soon as I reached him, he grabbed my bag, his arm brushing against my stomach as he scooped it off me. My skin tingled where he'd touched me and I sucked in my breath. Ack! What was my problem? So he accidentally touched me?

Get over it, Lily. Private lessons with Rafe meant nothing. Nothing!

My mom dropped me off at Keith's house at a quarter past two the next day. As soon as I got out of the car and away from my mom, I yanked off my T-shirt. I was wearing my new bikini under a pair of low-rider denim shorts and a camisole, cropped just enough to show off my belly-button ring.

My heart was thudding as I stood outside the front door. I should have snagged a ride from Erin, but my mom had insisted on driving me herself so she could see the house and make sure there were no kegs of beer sitting on the front lawn.

I glanced back at her. She waved at me from the car, waiting for a glimpse of a parental unit. How embarrassing.

I took a deep breath and then rang the doorbell.

Keith's mom opened the door. She was wearing a bikini with a towel wrapped around her waist and sunglasses perched on her head. For a mom, she looked pretty good in the bikini, actually. She smiled at me. "You must be here for Keith's party."

"Um, yeah. I'm Lily." I felt my cheeks heat up. "Can you, like, wave at my mom or something?"

Keith's mom looked past me toward the street. "I'll just run out there and say hello." She pulled the door open wider. "Just head straight down the hall to the back of the house and go out the sliding glass doors to the backyard."

"Okay." I hugged my towel to my chest and headed back. If my friends weren't there yet, I was going to go hide in the bathroom until they arrived. No *way* was I going to go out there by myself.

I walked to the back of the house, toward the sound of splashing, my heart racing. What was I doing here? I didn't know anyone. I didn't belong. I . . . I needed a date for the semi.

The semi.

I stopped in the doorway and stared out at the pool. There were four guys and three girls in the water, playing Marco Polo. My friends, and the guys from Inverness. Including Les.

Erin saw me and waved. "Lily! Come on in! The water's great!"

She was wearing her new bikini, and she looked awesome. Tan and everything.

The guys were all in bathing suits too. Everyone was in bathing suits. Well, duh. It was a pool party, right?

I stepped onto the patio, still hugging my towel. "Hey, guys." Yikes. How shaky was my voice?

Erin shrieked suddenly and went flying straight up in the air before landing with a splash three feet away. Some guy came out of the water where she'd been, grinning as water cascaded down his face. "Got you!"

She spluttered to the surface. "Keith! You're such a jerk!" But she was grinning as she checked the coverage of her top.

"Oh!" Val exclaimed. "Now that Lily's here, we have to do chicken fights."

"I get Val." A guy I assumed was Hugh

disappeared under the water and then came up again, with Val on his shoulders.

She grabbed his head and hooked her feet behind his back. "I guess I'm partners with Hugh."

Oh, God. Was I going to have to sit on Les's shoulders? I couldn't do it. I—

"Coming, Lily?"

I looked down to see Les standing in the water, looking up at me. He was muscular and his hair was sticking up from where he'd flipped the water out of it. He was actually pretty cute. Not as cute as Rafe, but decent. And he was looking at me as though he might actually like me. I looked down at him. "Do you have a girl-friend?"

His eyes widened. "No."

Point for him. He was available. But I hugged my towel even tighter.

"Do you have a boyfriend?" he asked.

"Uh . . ." I quickly surveyed the pool and noticed that Val was eavesdropping.

His eyes got even wider. "You do?"

Crud. This wasn't going to help me get a date to the semi, was it?

A sudden grin lit up his face. "Lily of many surprises. I like that."

I blinked. He liked the fact I had a boy-friend?

Then I felt like smacking my head. Of course he would. If some other guy liked me, then there must be something good about me, right? Guys were such pains in the butt.

"Coming in?" he asked.

"I just have to find a place for my towel. . . ."

"I'll take it." His eyes were glittering now with interest. What? To see me in a bikini? Ha. As if he'd get the chance.

"No, I'll just . . ."

He pulled himself up on the edge of the pool. "Come here. I have to ask you some-thing."

I got even more nervous. Was he going to ask me right now? To the semi? I bit my lip and leaned toward him. "What?"

He suddenly grabbed my wrist and yanked

115

me off balance. I shrieked, but I had no chance as I flew over his head and crashed into the water. What a *jerk*! I stood up and wiped the water out of my eyes. "Les!"

But I couldn't see him anywhere.

Then suddenly I felt something brush against my legs, but before I could move away, he stood up right under me, forcing me to sit on his shoulders. He wrapped his hands around my legs and flipped the water out of his eyes. "We're ready."

I clutched at his head, my heart thudding. I could feel his bare shoulders against my legs. His skin was wet and warm and I was completely *freaking out here*! I didn't want to be on his shoulders! I didn't want his hands on my legs! "Put me down!"

"No way. We're going to win." He sloshed through the water toward Val. "I'll try to take out Hugh and you go for Val's top."

"You want me to rip off her bikini? Are you *kidding*?" I was so glad I still had my shirt on!

"She'll let go of Hugh to keep it on, and

then they'll go down." His fingers tightened around my legs and I wanted to kick him.

"My *boyfriend* would be completely ticked if he saw you grabbing me like this," I hissed as he advanced on Val and Hugh. Erin and Delilah were already going at it with their battle.

"Well, then, it's a good thing he's not here, isn't it?" We reached Val and began circling them.

I looked at Val. "Let's do something else, Val. I don't want to—" She grabbed my arm and yanked me sideways. "Hey!"

Les cursed and jumped to the left to stay under me. "Come on, Lily! Don't take that!"

I glared at Val. "Cut it out!"

"No!" She laughed and lunged for me again. I ducked and grabbed her wrist. Les took out one of Hugh's legs and I pulled, and suddenly they were going over. Les held up his arms in victory as Val and Hugh disappeared under the water in a splash, and I clung to Les's head to keep from falling off.

"We rule!" he crowed. He held up his hand

for a high five, and I reluctantly smacked it.

I wished Rafe were here. I wished it were Rafe whose shoulders I was on.

Too bad for me, right?

Chapter Ten

An hour and a half later, I was lying on a lounge chair next to Erin, catching some rays for the first time since last summer. The guys were cooking burgers on the grill and not paying us any attention, which was a relief.

Since they were at the other end of the pool, I'd finally given in to Erin's pressure to take off my camisole. I'd kept my clothes on the whole time I was in the pool—getting thrown in while dressed had been the perfect excuse. But tanning in my shirt didn't make sense.

I was keeping my shorts on, though. I'd

noticed that Erin had put hers back on too, so I didn't feel so bad.

Val and Delilah were helping the boys with the grill, wearing their bikinis and nothing else. Didn't they feel naked? No way could I do that. *Well, maybe if Rafe were here . . .* Argh! *Stop thinking about Rafe!*

"So, has Les asked you yet?" Erin asked.

"No." At least I hadn't had to make conversation with him. Getting tossed in the water repeatedly had taken care of any awkward silences. "Did Keith ask you?"

"Yes! Isn't that awesome?"

"Great." I stared across the pool at Les. He was laughing with Val, having a great time. They all looked like they were having so much fun, but I still felt so awkward. I didn't even really want to go to the dance with Les. Not really. But I couldn't stand the thought of staying home by myself.

"So, Rafe's way hot."

I grinned at Erin. "I know."

"Are you sure you can't get him to come to the semi?" She propped herself up on her elbow and shielded her eyes against the sun. "I mean, Les is cute, but why would you go with him if you could go with Rafe?"

I tensed. "I want to hang with you guys at the semi. Quadruple date."

She eyed me. "Why would you want to hang with us when you can be with Rafe? I mean, he's completely hot."

"I spend a lot of time with him." I pretended to inspect my toenails, which I'd painted fluorescent orange last night. "Especially now that I'm in his band." I shot her a sly look. "He's giving me private lessons to help me learn the music."

Her eyes widened. "So, is he a great kisser or what?"

"Ah . . ." *Oh, way to go, Lily. Can't you think before you open your mouth sometimes?*

"Want a hot dog?"

I looked up to see Les blocking my sun, holding a couple hot dogs. "Definitely."

Erin harrumphed, then leaned back in her chair and closed her eyes. Les sat down on my chair, and I had to jerk my feet away from him to keep him from sitting on them. He handed me the hot dog. "So, is who a good kisser? Your boyfriend?"

I took a bite of the hot dog instead of answering. This was so wrong!

"How come he's not taking you to the semi?"

I swallowed. "Because he's . . . um . . ." What would sound good? "He's got an audition."

"For what?"

"MTV."

Erin sat up. "What? You didn't tell us that! Since when?"

"They're doing another *Making the Band* show, and they need a drummer. Mueller-Fordham always sends a couple kids to those auditions." Well, they always sent kids to auditions for all the top classical programs in the country, as Erin knew. It wasn't that much of a stretch that Mueller-Fordham would also be asked to contribute to *Making the Band*. Top music schools got noticed, end of story. I knew Erin would buy it. "Rafe got the nod this time.

He's flying down to New York for the week-end."

Les's mouth dropped open. "He's going to be on MTV?"

"Yeah, but he might not make the actual show." I took another bite.

Erin sighed. "Of course he'll get picked. He's completely *hot*. Can you imagine? Your boyfriend will be like world famous!"

Les leaned over and rested his arm across my knees, which I'd propped up in front of me.

I glared at him. "My boyfriend wouldn't appreciate that." I wiggled my legs to get him off, but he didn't move. I really didn't want him touching me. I mean, he wasn't doing anything, not really, but all I could think of was Rafe.

Rafe with the girlfriend, remember?

I decided not to make Les move after all.

He grinned. "So what? He's not around to protect his territory. If you were my girlfriend, I'd be hanging out with you all the time. No guy would get a chance to talk to you."

Erin gave me a thumbs-up from behind Les, then she hopped to her feet and headed off toward the grill, leaving the two of us alone.

Uh-oh. I was going to have to talk again, wasn't I? I really wasn't good at that.

"So, Lily."

"So, Les." I took another bite of my hot dog and decided to chew for a long time. Like really long. Hey, it would be rude to talk with my mouth full, right?

He tapped his fingers against my shin. "You want to go to the semi with me?"

I froze mid-chew, then swallowed the whole lump in one go. My heart was pounding and I felt light-headed. "You don't care I have a boyfriend?"

He grinned and flicked my bangs off my forehead with his free hand. "It's just a dance, right? No big deal."

But there was a gleam in his eye that made my toes curl, and I wasn't sure if it was a good curl or a bad one.

"So? Want to go?"

I took another bite of my hot dog and chewed slowly, watching him, pretending to play hard to get while I frantically tried to get my thoughts together. Should I go with him? I should, right? I mean, it wasn't like Rafe was going to suddenly free up and be able to go with me. And even if he was single, he wasn't the semiformal type of guy. But what if he was? What if he'd go if I asked? But could I ask him? I couldn't. Could I? No, he had a girl-friend. But what if I invited him as friends? But then what? I'd be trapped in my original lie. Les was my chance to get another guy so I could "dump" Rafe.

"Lily?" Les's grin had faded and he was studying me intently. "Is that a no?"

I swallowed my hot dog. "No."

He frowned. "No, it's not a no, or no, you're not going to go with me?"

Okay, so I couldn't help it. It was kind of funny to see Les getting all worked up after I'd been so worried about impressing him that first day. I liked being in control way better. "Which do you think it is?"

He narrowed his eyes at me. "Are you mess-ing with me?"

"Yep."

"Messing with me as in you're about to say no, or messing with me as in you're planning to say yes, but you're torturing me first?"

"Exactly!" I grinned at the disgruntled look on his face.

He groaned. "Lily! Are you going with me or not?"

"Yes!"

He started to smile, then frowned. "Yes, you're going with me, or yes, you're not?"

I patted his cheek. "I need to check with my boyfriend. Call me tomorrow night and I'll let you know, okay?"

He looked surprised. "Playing hard to get?"

"I *am* hard to get." *Oh, good one, Lily.*

He grinned and trailed his fingers over my knee, his eyes bright with interest that hadn't been there the day we'd met on the field. "I'll call you. Definitely." Then he stood up and walked back toward the grill.

I flopped my arms over my head and watched everyone flirting over by the grill. I was the only one not over there. I should have felt good, right? I mean, Les was into me. I could quadruple date with my friends. I'd established my social status for my entire high school career.

But I didn't feel good. Not at all.

Les only liked me because he thought I had a boyfriend. What would happen when he found out I didn't? Would he ditch me and run away again?

I was cool only because I had a fake boyfriend. A fake boyfriend with a fake MTV audition. A fake boyfriend who had a real girlfriend. A fake boyfriend who I couldn't stop thinking about. I was so in over my head.

Chapter Eleven

For the whole ride to Mueller-Fordham, from the minute Rafe picked me up on Sunday morning to the moment we got into the rehearsal room, all he did was talk about the band's music.

And all I could do was think about how much cuter he was than Les. How he probably wouldn't throw me in the pool with all my clothes on, unless he knew I'd be okay with it.

He was wearing a Red Sox hat, a pair of khaki shorts with all sorts of cool pockets on them, and a faded red shirt that looked like bleach had gotten splashed on it. He was so different from Les and the rest of the Inverness guys.

Rafe was *real*.

"Are you listening?"

I blinked and stared at him. He was sitting at his drums and I was standing at the keyboard. "Um, I sort of tuned out for a minute."

"I asked if you were ready to play."

I sighed. "Um, no. I need to practice on my own for a sec." I forced myself to look at the sheet music that he'd given me after our last practice. I'd messed around with it a bit, and it wasn't so hard. I played a few bars, then I looked up at Rafe. "Good?"

To my surprise, he shook his head. "This isn't classical. You need to put some energy into it."

I felt myself tense up. "There's energy."

"No, there isn't. Listen." He played a few bars on his drums. Simple, fine. "Now, compare that to this." He played the exact same bars, but it was different. Buzzing with energy, vibrating. "See the difference?"

I pursed my lips. "Yeah."

"So, do it like that."

I nodded, and played it again, then looked up. I bit my lip when I saw Rafe shaking his head again. "What's wrong now?"

"You just played it louder. Louder isn't better. Play it like you play the JamieX song."

My head was starting to hurt, but I sang a few lines of the JamieX song, then played the new song again.

This time I didn't need to look at Rafe to know it wasn't enough. I dropped my hands and stepped back, my throat tight as all the old pressures slammed into me. "You know, I think the band thing isn't a good idea."

Rafe rested his drumsticks on his thigh. "Why are you freaking out? So you can't get the song right yet. So what? That's what practice is for."

"No. It's that stupid passion thing." I started shaking my head and backing toward the door. "I just don't have it. This is why I quit the piano. Why I'm not doing the audition. Because I can't." I was babbling now, but I didn't care. "I have to leave. I just have to get out."

"Where are you going?"

I didn't answer him. I simply yanked open the door and sprinted down the hall.

"Lily!"

Rafe caught up to me as I vaulted down the stairs and landed on the lawn. He jumped after me and his momentum sent him slamming into me and we both sprawled onto the grass. I rolled onto my back and stared at the sky—the stupid blue sky.

"Sorry." He propped himself up on his elbow and peered down at me. "I didn't mean to tackle you. You okay?"

"Fine. It's my weekend for being tackled by guys, apparently." I suddenly realized his face was right over mine. Like, his lips were inches from my face. All he had to do was lean over a little and . . . I squeezed my eyes shut and sighed. "Go away."

"What audition?"

"NorthEast Seminary of Music secondary school program." I peeked out of my left eye, and he was still leaning over me. So close I

could smell his cologne or aftershave or whatever it was. It didn't matter what it was. It simply smelled amazing. So I closed my eyes again.

"Are you kidding? You got an audition for
NESM? That's awesome."

A bubble of pride popped up at his genuine
admiration, but I immediately popped it. "No,
because I'm going to fail at it and embarrass
your aunt and my family. So I'm not going."

I felt a tap on my forehead. I opened my
eyes. "What?"

His hair had flopped over his forehead in
that totally cute way it always did. "You're really
not going?"

"Really." I waited for him to tell me I was
throwing my future away. To tell me what an
idiot I was. To tell me that refusing to try was
the worst kind of failure.

But all he did was flop on his back, his
shoulder resting against mine. "Cool."

This time I propped myself up on my elbow
and peered down at him. "Cool? How?"

His green eyes flicked toward me. "Cool

that you're doing your own thing. If you're not ready, then it's good not to do it."

"Really? You mean that?"

"Sure."

"Oh." I laid back down, no longer touching him. I mean, I wanted to, but I wasn't exactly going to scoot across the grass so I could.

Instead, he shifted until his head was resting against mine. "You're wrong, you know."

Here it comes. "For not doing the audition?"

"No, for thinking you don't have passion. You do when you play the JamieX song."

I tried not to think about the fact that his head was resting against mine. "But I can't create it."

"Don't try. Just have fun."

I frowned. "Music isn't about fun."

He immediately leaned over me. This time he was wicked close, so close I could smell his toothpaste. Mint. "What did you just say?"

Um, good question. I was having a little trouble thinking with his mouth so close to mine. What if Rafe was my first kiss? That would be so amazing. . . .

"You think music's not about fun?"

Oh, right. I *had* said something about that. "It's work," I explained. "It's a career. It's not fun."

He shook his head and made a face. "You are so wrong, babe."

Babe? I was his babe? Oh. My. God.

"You and me. Tuesday night. We have a date."

I blinked. "A date?"

Something flashed over his face. "Well, not a *date*, date."

"Because you have a girlfriend." Stupid girlfriend.

"And you have a boyfriend."

The words hung in the air, and for a moment, with him still staring down at me, I wanted to tell him the truth. To see if he'd care. To see if it would change anything.

Then he rolled away from me and stood up, breaking the connection. "Come on, Lily. We have some songs to learn."

"No, I can't. Didn't you hear what I said? I'm horrible and I'm going to mess it up for the rest of the band."

Rafe grabbed my hand and pulled me to my feet. "Today, you're going to worry only about learning the music for our gig at the middle school on Saturday. Forget about passion and all that other junk. Just learn the music, okay? You can do that, right?"

I nodded. "Well, yeah, but—"

He put his hand over my mouth, and my knees nearly gave out. "Don't say it, Lily. Learn the music. That's all. Okay?"

If I didn't nod, how long would he leave his hand over my mouth?

"Lily?"

Fine. I nodded, and he dropped his hand. Total bummer. Why hadn't I been that bummed when Les had stopped touching me?

Rafe brushed my back and directed me toward the school. "Tuesday night, Lily, you're going to find out exactly how much fun music can be."

Tuesday night. Oh, *wow*. I had a date with Rafe.

Okay, not a *date*, but a date. What if he sort of liked me? What if I didn't have to go to the semi with Les? What if I said yes to Les tonight and then on Tuesday Rafe said he liked me? Like *liked* me. I sneaked a peek at Rafe as we walked back up the steps.

"Um, Rafe?"

"Yeah?" He opened the door for me.

"There's this semiformal at school in two weeks and um, if I needed a date, like if I was desperate, and it wouldn't really be a date or anything, but you know, well, would you like maybe go with me, like if I needed a favor or something like that?"

He froze and stared at me. *"What?"*

Oh, God! Had I really just invited him? Did I have absolutely *no* control over my mouth?

He looked totally shocked, and I knew I'd blown it. I'd crossed that line of friendship and he was going to have to let me down easy and I would be so embarrassed that I'd never be able to look at him again and everything would be awkward around us forever and ever and everyone in the band would be able to tell and they would know that I'd thrown myself at him and he'd had to ditch me . . . I was such an idiot!

"Never mind. Forget it." My cheeks burning, I ducked under his arm and bolted for the rehearsal room.

I was already playing the keyboard when he walked in. Was he going to say something? Was he going to say that he'd like to go? I mean, it was out there now. He could pick up on it if he wanted to. I peered at him under the shield of my hair.

He glanced at me, and my heart skipped a beat. What was he going to say? His cheeks were flushed and he looked a little nervous. Unsettled. He was going to tell me he was going to go, wasn't he?

He took a breath. "You ready to learn some tunes?"

"Tunes?" I echoed. *Tunes?*

"Yeah. Today's about learning the music, remember?"

I'd just asked him to my semiformal, and he wanted to talk about music.

My life was *over*.

Chapter Twelve XOXOX

Erin called me at eight thirty that night. "So? Did Les call?"

"No." I was lying on my bed, listening to JamieX. I should have been practicing the songs for the band. Or doing my homework.

But all I could think about was how awkward the entire practice had been with Rafe. He'd barely looked at me and he'd made sure not to touch me, not even accidentally. It was horrible.

"Good. I think you should ask Rafe again. He's so hot. MTV? Are you kidding? He's going to become the next superstar! You think your parents will let you go on tour with him? I mean, that would be awesome. I could come visit you and—"

"I asked him. He can't go." I propped my feet up on the wall and stared at my JamieX poster. Even JamieX wasn't as cute as Rafe.

"Wow. Sucks. So, then it's Les, huh?"

I sighed. "He hasn't called."

"Oh, he'll call. I was talking to Keith tonight, and he said Les couldn't stop talking about you after the party. He loved your belly-button ring. Said it rocked."

I eyed my toes. I should redo them. Maybe black. Yes, black would be good. No cheerful colors anymore.

"Lily? Did you hear me? Les has the hots for you."

"Yeah." I didn't have black toenail polish. I'd have to go buy some tomorrow.

Call waiting beeped, and my heart jumped. I took the phone away from my ear and looked at the display. J. Jespersen. *Please let it be Rafe, not Miss Jespersen.* "Rafe's beeping in. I gotta go." I clicked over even as Erin was ordering me to call her after Les called me. "Hello?"

"Hey, Lily. It's Rafe."

My throat caught. "What's up?"

"I forgot to tell you that we don't have practice tomorrow night. I'm going out with Paige. I kinda gotta do that since I'm not seeing her at practice anymore."

I sagged into my pillows. "Oh."

"But you can practice on your own, right? I mean, you know the music enough?"

"Sure."

He cleared his throat. "So, um, I'll pick you up at seven on Tuesday?"

"For our non-date, date."

He hesitated. "Um, yeah."

"Can't wait."

"Um, Lily—"

"I gotta go. Dinner. See you Tuesday." I hung up before he could bring up the semi. The most embarrassing moment of my life. I ask him to the dance and then he calls twelve hours later to remind me that he's got a date with his real girlfriend? Major humiliation.

The phone rang again and I answered it on the first ring. "What?"

"Lily?"

I frowned. It was a guy's voice that I didn't recognize. "Chris?" Maybe the band was going to have practice without Rafe.

"No, it's Les. Who's Chris? I thought your boyfriend's name is Rafe."

"Chris is my other boyfriend."

"Really? You have two?"

I rolled my eyes at the excitement in his voice. He was so going to lose interest when he found out I had no boyfriends. "What's up, Les?"

"So, the semi. You said you'd give me an answer tonight."

I hesitated. What choice did I have? I had to have a life, and Les was asking.

"Lily? Don't leave me hanging."

"Yes, I'll go."

"Excellent." His voice was mellow, but loaded with satisfaction.

I sighed. Why wasn't I more excited? I

mean, he was cute, he was a sophomore, and he liked me. Or, at least, he liked who he thought I was. Close enough to heaven, right?

"So, the guys are thinking about renting a stretch limo for the four couples. Sound good?"

I perked up. "Really? A limo?" I'd never been in a limo before.

"Yeah. Like, dinner first, then the dance? Then maybe back to Keith's for an afterparty? Some midnight swimming and stuff?"

And stuff. I didn't like the sound of that. Not at all. I mean, Keith's mom had never come out the whole time we'd been at the pool. What about at night? When his parents were asleep? What kind of *stuff* did he have in mind?

I suddenly got really nervous.

"So, should the limo come by your place or are you girls going to meet at one house?"

I blinked. "Erin's. You can pick me up at Erin's." As if I was getting into that limo by myself.

"Got it. How about five?"

"Sure."

"Okay, then. Gotta run."

I hung up and tossed the phone at the pillow. Great. My life was great. I had Les by the ankles. No piano. No audition. Everything was perfect.

So how come I was so depressed?

Chapter Thirteen XOXOX

By Tuesday night, I was a wreck. I'd practiced the band music until I had it perfectly memorized, but I could tell it was heavy and dull. I'd spent all day at school on Monday and Tuesday discussing semi plans with my friends, and getting more and more worried about the afterparty.

My only hope was to have my parents ban me from going, and it almost worked. Mom had freaked because the semi was the night before the audition, but Dad had been like, "She needs to go."

I mean, yeah, great, because that meant he'd accepted I wasn't going to the audition, but *man*! I didn't want to deal with that afterparty! On the other hand, it wasn't like I could say no. I'd barely ditched my loser rep. If I bailed on the party because I didn't want to go, then I'd be right back to loserdom again.

And Rafe. *Ugh.* I couldn't deal with seeing him. Total embarrassment.

I'd thought about canceling our Tuesday-night "date." I even picked up the phone to call him once. But in the end, I couldn't. And it wasn't just the thought of seeing him. It was his promise that music could be fun. I had to know if he was right.

Rafe was five minutes early. I saw his Jeep pull up, and I jumped off my bed and raced down the stairs, yanking the door open just as he was raising his hand to knock. He looked startled. Crud. Now he knew I was watching for him. I blinked in feigned surprise.

"Rafe? I was just going outside to check the mail. Is it time already?"

He nodded, his eyes scanning the outfit that I'd spent three hours picking out. A short skirt, my Uggs, and a black top that showed off my sunburn from the pool party and my navel ring. His gaze lingered on my stomach for an instant, and I felt myself heat up.

"Belly-button ring?" he asked. "You don't seem the type."

Oh . . . I was so going to melt under that look. Especially since he looked so hot in a pair of black jeans, a black T-shirt, and black boots. He was wearing a black leather jacket and his hair was a little messy. He was also wearing a knotted leather necklace with a metal horse-shoe. My parents would freak. Bad boy all the way. I grinned. "Don't tell my parents about my belly-button ring."

"They don't know?"

"Nope." I tied a sweater around my waist. "See? It's hidden."

He grinned. "Such a rebel."

"Hey, you told me to blow off adults, right?"

"Mmm . . ."

"Mom!" I shouted. "Rafe's here! We're leaving!"

"Hang on!" A pot clanged in the kitchen, and then my mom walked out, wiping her hands on her jeans. Dad was right behind her. Mom eyed Rafe, her gaze sweeping over his outfit. "So, you're Miss Jespersen's nephew." She sounded skeptical. Why not? He didn't exactly look like he had Crusty's uptight blood running through him.

"Yes, ma'am." He shook her hand, and then my dad's. "Rafe Turner. Nice to meet you both. I won't keep Lily out too late, and I have a cell phone with me if you need to reach us. I can leave the number if you like."

My dad raised his brows at me and I felt my cheeks heat up. Rafe was acting like the perfect date. Like he was trying to impress my parents.

My mom's face softened and she smiled. "Yes, a phone number would be great."

"No problem." He took a pen and paper from my dad and jotted it down. "The show goes until ten, so we should be back by ten thirty. Is that all right?"

Show? We were going to a show?

My mom frowned. "It's a little late for a school night."

"What show?" my dad asked.

"We're going to a piano bar."

A *piano* bar? What was that?

"Oh." My dad put his arm around my mom, a strange smile on his face. "No problem. Have fun."

"We will." Rafe shook their hands again and then held the door for me.

Twenty minutes later, Rafe knocked on the side door of a bar in downtown Boston. A bar! We were actually going to a bar! And my parents had agreed! "Aren't we going to get in trouble? It's not like we're twenty-one."

He grinned. "It's not that kind of bar."

Right. It was a piano bar. I wasn't sure if I liked the sound of that. . . .

The door was opened by a gorgeous woman. She wore a black silk dress and high heels and exuded class and sophistication. She smiled at us, her eyes bright but a little wary. "It's so good to see you, Rafe." She reached out and hugged him, but I saw Rafe tense just before she grabbed him.

Who was she?

She looked at me. "And who's your little friend?"

Rafe put his arm around me. "This is Lily. She's a piano player. Lily, this is my mom."

His mom? As in the one who'd ditched him? No *way*.

"How lovely! Maybe she'll play for us tonight."

I froze. "Um, sorry, but I'm retired."

The woman smiled and touched my cheek, in the same way Rafe had done. "Of course." She stepped back. "Come on back. The doors won't officially open for another twenty minutes, so feel free to wander around." She trailed her fingers through Rafe's hair, giving him a sad look; then she turned and strode off into the back of the club.

"Sitting up front's best." Rafe cleared his throat and started walking through the club.

There were tables everywhere, with little candles in the middle of each one. And along the sides of the room were black pianos. Five on each side and two grand pianos at the front. They were on risers, so they were a couple feet off the ground. The ceiling was pretty high and sort of curved, with all sorts of wooden carvings. Very interesting and unique, actually. "What is this place?" I asked, relaxing slightly.

"You'll see." Rafe sat down at a table in the second row, right in the middle. "This is my favorite table."

I sat next to him, and scanned the room. There were people running around, shouting and getting things organized. It was a frantic kind of energy, but not a bad one. Sort of excited and fun. One guy tossed a bundle of napkins over our head, and someone else caught it and sprinted off, hollering at another guy. I smiled. "This place is cool."

"Yeah."

A woman in a maroon vest and white shirt came over and set a couple waters, two sodas, and a plate of veggies and chips in front of us. "Good to see you, Rafe. It's been a while."

"Thanks, Rosie." He grinned at her.

As he picked up his drink, I eyed him. "You come here a lot?"

He shrugged. "I used to. My mom and dad own the place, so it's basically where I grew up."

I inspected the room more carefully. This was Rafe's parents' place? "Where's your dad?"

"Probably hiding out back. They try to avoid each other, since they can't be in the same room without screaming at each other." The bitterness in his voice made me look back at him, but he was glaring at something invisible on the stage. "I stopped coming when this place became a war zone."

"Oh." I couldn't imagine my parents fighting like that. Rafe's shoulders were all tense and his jaw was clenched. Without thinking about it, I touched the back of his hand. "That sucks."

He glanced at my hand on his, then looked

at me, without moving out of my reach. "Yeah, it does."

"How long has it been since you were last here?"

He flipped his hand over so his palm was against mine, and curled his fingers through mine, his thumb rubbing on my palm. "Since the day they told me they were getting a divorce. About eighteen months."

My hand felt so warm in his. Just, like, perfect. "That's forever. Didn't you miss it?"

"Yeah, but I didn't want to come here and watch my parents scream at each other."

"I can see that."

We fell silent for a moment, and I watched a woman fix a bouquet that was on the stage between the two pianos. "So, how come you're here now?"

"Because I wanted to bring you here."

"Oh." I was going to die, but I forced myself not to gape at him. So I looked around, suddenly realizing that the room was filling up with patrons. It was getting loud and rowdy,

and people were laughing and having fun. Then I sat up and stared at the woman across the room. She was wearing jeans and a sparkly red top, and she was talking to Rafe's mom. *Laughing* with Rafe's mom. She almost looked like . . .

"Rafe? Is that your aunt?"

He followed my glance, then nodded. "Yeah, she's a regular here on Tuesday nights."

"Really?" I watched her as she turned to an attractive older guy wearing jeans and a polo shirt. She said something to him to make him laugh; then she tucked her arm through his. "She looks so normal. I never thought of her as having a life outside of the music school. Is that her *boyfriend*?"

"Yeah. He's a firefighter."

"No way! Crusty's dating someone who gets dirty for a living?" Unbelievable. How could this be the same woman who tortured me daily?

"I told you, she's pretty cool. She's the one who gave me permission to get a tattoo. My parents never would have." He turned toward me suddenly and leaned on the table, his hand still around mine, like he'd forgotten about it or something. "I have to ask you something."

I felt my throat tighten at the intensity of his expression, and I immediately put Crusty out of my mind. "What?"

"On Sunday, were you asking me to go to your semiformal with you?"

I pressed my lips together. What answer did he want? "I . . ."

"Isn't your boyfriend going with you?"

"Well . . ."

Rafe was still waiting for an answer.

Crud. What should I say? I mean, was I going to admit I'd lied the whole time?

"Don't you have a date?"

"Well, I guess, but I just said yes last night because, well . . ."

Something glittered in his eyes. "You really did ask me."

"No." I snorted and pulled my hand free. "I was just asking in case I needed to ask later.

Like if my date got run over by a bus or something."

"You really think I'd fit in at a semiformal for St. Mary's?"

I looked right at him. "You'd fit in anywhere you wanted to fit."

He gave me a long stare.

I shifted under his gaze. "What?"

"Does your boyfriend go to Inverness?"

Here was my chance to tell him Les wasn't my boyfriend. But what was the point? He just took Paige out last night. She wasn't fake and I didn't want Rafe to reject me. I lifted my chin. "Les is a sophomore there. Plays lacrosse."

"Ah. A lacrosse player." He gave me a speculative look. "I wouldn't think you were the type to be into a lacrosse player."

I'm not. "What's my type? You?"

He blinked. "What? Why would you say that?"

Oh, God. Had I really just said that? "Yeah, you're the nephew of the woman put on this earth to torture me. My dream guy."

His gaze narrowed. "You judge me for being

Aunt Joyce's nephew?"

No. I think you're perfect. Like I could say that. "She hates me."

Rafe frowned. "She doesn't hate you." He looked around, then leaned forward until his lips were only an inch from my ear. "Don't tell my parents, but she saved me when they freaked out, Lily. She's tough, but without her . . ." He paused and I looked at him. His face was so close to mine, all I'd have to do is lean forward and then our lips . . .

Then I noticed his eyes. They were so sad. So incredibly lonely.

I touched his cheek, and he grabbed my hand and held it against his face. "Without her, I'd have lost it. Give her a chance to help you, too, Lily. It's all she wants to do."

I tried to understand what he was saying. She had talked my mom into giving me a break from lessons, and she was here tonight, right? Besides, if Rafe liked her, then she had to be okay, didn't she?

The lights suddenly dimmed and Rafe's mom walked out on stage. "I'd like to welcome you to our traditional Tuesday night Battle of the Ivories."

Rafe and I turned toward the stage, and I felt Rafe lean back in his chair and rest his arm over the back of mine. Probably because it was more comfortable like that. Not because he was making a move. Right. It was good I was going to the semi with Les. Whatever it would take for me to stop thinking about Rafe.

He squeezed my shoulder to get my attention, then winked at me. "You're about to see how fun piano can be," he whispered.

"Impossible," I whispered back.

Then I heard a furious burst of music from my left and I spun around. A guy in black leather and a mohawk was at the piano, thrashing at the keys. It was the most amazing music I'd ever heard—fast and frenzied and crazy. I listened in shocked awe. Then he slammed the final chord, and before it had faded, music jumped at me from my other side.

The whole crowd spun back to the right, where a woman in a navy suit started in at another piano. "Wow! She's amazing." I leaned past Rafe, trying to get closer to her.

He grinned and rested his arm across my back as I leaned over him. "Just wait. It gets better."

"No way." And then just like that, she stopped playing, and music started up on my left side. I whipped around again, and the spotlight was on the first piano. There was an old guy with gray hair pounding away at the keys. He stood up, dancing and swaying as he charged through his song, power exploding from his body and from the music.

Then he stopped and the second piano on the right was lit up. I nearly fell on top of Rafe in my effort to see who was playing, to catch a glimpse of whoever was next. "That's your mom!"

Rafe was playing the piano on my back, tapping his left foot in beat with the music. "Yeah. She's good, huh?"

"Unbelievable!"

Then the music burst from the other side

and I spun around again. "I've never heard piano like this! It's like they're talking to each other!"

"That's why it's called the Battle of the Ivories." He nudged me and pointed to the sandy-haired man pouring out the music. "That's my dad."

I bounced on the edge of my seat. "No wonder you're such an amazing musician! You're descended from greatness."

He glanced at me. "You think I'm amazing?"

"God, yes! So much better than anyone else at Mueller-Fordham!" I spun around as the third piano on the right started playing. I leaned across him again, letting the music consume me. It was fast and energetic and raging with power. It was alive! All of it! People were shouting and clapping and cheering and some were even on their feet. Because of piano! Out of the corner of my eye, I saw even Crusty jumping up and down and shouting. "This is so amazing. Incredible. I can't believe it!"

The instant Rafe's dad finished, I jumped to my feet with half a dozen other people and started applauding like mad, even as the next pianist leaped into the fray. Rafe stood up, cheering loudly as well. He grinned at me. "Having fun?"

"This rocks!" I threw my arms around his neck and hugged him, my body vibrating with excitement. More people jumped to their feet when the next pianist began to play. "This is the best night of my life!"

His arms went around my waist and suddenly I realized what I was doing. I was hanging on to him. I pulled back, but he didn't let go. And then we were staring at each other, his arms holding me against him, my fingers in the hair at the back of his neck. All I could do was stare at him, my heart thumping.

For the longest time, we just stood there, in the midst of all these people. All I could think is that I wanted him to kiss me more than I'd ever wanted anything in my whole life.

His gaze dropped to my mouth, and my

stomach did a triple flip. Was he really going to kiss me? Right there? In front of all those people?

Then he cleared his throat, dropped his hands from my waist, and stepped back.

I immediately yanked my hands out of his hair and clenched my fists at my sides.

We stared at each other for another long moment, and then we both shook it off and turned at the same time to face the pianist who was currently playing.

There wasn't a single touch between us the rest of the night—not even an accidental one. But it was still the best night of my life.

Chapter Fourteen

I went straight home and sat down at the piano and tried to imitate what I'd heard that night. I ditched the classical and the rock and just pounded away, going crazy with whatever felt like flying off my fingers. My mom popped her head in once, and I stopped, thinking she was going to tell me to knock it off because it was so late. But all she did was smile, shut the windows so the neighbors wouldn't be bothered, and go back upstairs.

So I kept playing.

After an hour, I was drenched in sweat, my

heart was racing, and I was completely pumped. It was *awesome*.

I couldn't remember the last time piano had made me sweat, except from stress.

At midnight, I pulled out the music from the band and started working on that, closing my eyes and pretending I was at the piano bar and everyone was screaming and dancing and clapping.

At one o'clock in the morning, I swiped Rafe's cell phone number from the slip of paper he'd left for my parents and called him. He'd understand how pumped I was.

He answered on the third ring. "Yeah?" His voice was groggy and sleepy and I almost hung up. "Who's this?"

"It's . . . Lily."

"Oh, hey." I heard the smile in his voice. "What's up?" He cleared his throat and I heard him rustling around.

I grinned and ran my fingers over the keys. "I just wanted to say thanks for tonight. It was awesome. I've been messing around on the piano since I got home. It's fun."

"Told you."

"Yeah, well, you were right."

"I'm always right."

"You're a dork," I said with a laugh. "So, I'll see you at practice tomorrow?"

"You mean today?"

"Yeah, today." I paused, suddenly not sure what else I was going to say. "So, I guess I'll go to bed." I started to hang up and then I heard him say my name, so I put the phone next to my ear. "What?"

"I had fun tonight too. Thanks for going with me."

"Sure."

"My mom called me when I got home. She liked you. Wants us to come back sometime."

I smiled. "I'd like that."

"She hasn't called me in weeks. I think she was glad we went."

God, how awful not to have your parents call you. "Anytime, Rafe."

He grunted. "Okay. See ya."

"Bye." I hung up and tapped the phone on my thigh. Why hadn't he ever taken Paige there? Why me?

Even though I was beat from my late night at the piano, rehearsal went great for the rest of the week. Every time I started to get uptight about the music, Rafe just reminded me about the Battle of the Ivories. I was able to remember everyone in the audience getting into it, and I'd relax again, reminding myself to have fun.

And it worked.

On Saturday night, by the time we were done setting up the instruments at the middle school for our performance, I was pumped to be there. It was so different to be prepping for a performance with other people. I had a team supporting me.

I wasn't alone!

Everyone in the band seemed to like me, the music was going well, and no one had mentioned Paige all week.

And Erin was going to try to get Val and Delilah to come watch the band tonight.

Finally, I was *cool*.

Angel sidled over to me, fiddling with her guitar. "So, Lily, what's up with you and Rafe?"

Heat flared into my cheeks as I looked up at her. "What do you mean?"

"I mean, what's up?"

"Nothing."

She snorted, and pretended to fiddle with her tuning. "You've been gawking at him all week in rehearsals, and you two keep having these little secret smiles."

Really? We had secret smiles? I grinned to myself and ducked my head. "Just playing music."

She grabbed my wrist and I looked up. She was studying me intently. "Rafe's a great guy. Don't mess with him."

"Me? He's the one with the girlfriend."

"And you're the one with the boyfriend." She let go of my wrist. "He's actually fun again, and if it's because of you . . ."

Me? I had no idea what to say. I wasn't sure if I could say anything.

"Lily? Do you like him?"

I bit my lip. "He has a girlfriend."

"What if he didn't?"

I felt my heart thud and I met her gaze. "He does, so there's no point, right? It doesn't matter what I think."

Her expression softened. "You *like* him!"

"No, I don't! That would be completely stupid and—"

"Hey, Rafe," she interrupted, looking over my shoulder.

I smacked my lips shut and felt my face heat up. I was *not* going to turn around.

But I did.

Rafe smiled at me, his eyes going all dark and sweeping over my outfit. "You look hot tonight. Not like a boring pianist."

I couldn't help but beam at him. Erin and I had spent all day working on my outfit. I'd borrowed a pair of black faux leather pants from her, and a sparkly gold camisole. I was wearing these awesome dangly earrings and a fake diamond in my belly-button piercing. I'd even done my hair with highlights and it rocked. And yeah, I'd bought a new bra, too. From

Victoria's Secret. It was black and had lace and silk and it was by far the sexiest thing I'd ever seen in my life.

Could Rafe sense I was wearing a new bra? Would he suddenly realize I was the girl of his dreams?

Not that I cared. He had a girlfriend. I. Didn't. Care.

Angel snickered at him. "If you'd stop gawking at her, maybe we could start to play?"

Rafe's face reddened and he turned away from me, toward the rest of the band. "You guys ready?"

Without waiting, he hopped behind his drums and started a beat. Nash and Angel came in, then I started playing, closing my eyes and wiggling my hips the way some of the piano players had at the bar.

Then Chris started singing and the place went nuts.

I snapped my eyes open, shocked to suddenly see tons of middle schoolers screaming and dancing and going crazy. Because of us.

Omigod. This was *so* cool.

So different than a recital, where everyone just sat around in silence, then applauded politely. This was *awesome*!

The dance ended way too soon, and the band all high-fived one another when we were done. Even Angel hugged me. Then, when she let go, Rafe came over and hugged me too. "You did great," he said, not letting go for a long time.

He was so warm and smelled so good. I beamed at him. "It's so fun!"

"Imagine that." He touched my cheek. "What a concept."

"Thanks to you."

He tangled his fingers in my hair as Chris bumped into me, but neither of us looked away from each other. Rafe kept his gaze fastened on my face. "I promised myself I wasn't going to say anything, but . . ."

"But, what?" *Say it, Rafe.* Was Angel right? Was he going to tell me he liked me? Ask me if I'd dump my boyfriend for him?

He tightened his fingers around the back of my neck. "I think you should do the audition."

I blinked. "What?"

"The audition. Don't go in there and play Mozart or Bach. Play music from the band. Play music that makes you come alive. You don't have to play classical to be great."

Angel and Nash high-fived each other, but I ignored them to stare at Rafe. "Why are you talking about the audition?"

"Because you're amazingly talented, Lily, and you deserve to be recognized. But do it on your own terms. Play what you like."

I felt a sudden ping of hope in my chest at the thought of going to the audition on my own terms. I would never have thought of it before, but tonight had been amazing. Tonight I had loved music. Was he right? "I don't want the pressure . . ."

"I'll drive you. We don't even need to tell my aunt or your parents. We'll just do it." His gaze was intense. "What time's the audition?"

"Ten."

"So, I'll pick you up at eight thirty. Next Saturday."

I shook my head. "No, I can't. I don't want to."

He nodded. "Whatever. If you want to, I'll go with you." He shrugged and tightened his fingers in my hair. "If you don't, that's cool too. I'll still . . ." He didn't finish.

I caught my breath. *You'll still what? Like me?*

"Lily!" Erin cried, rushing toward us from the crowd.

No! Not now! I ignored Erin's voice and didn't turn away from Rafe. "You'll still what?"

But Rafe looked away from me toward Erin and the moment was lost. Argh! I spun around to face Erin, and the grin dropped off my face when I saw she was standing there with not only Val and Delilah, but the guys from Inverness. Including Les. Who was watching Rafe intently.

Oh, *no*!

Rafe dropped his hand from my hair. "Friends of yours?"

"Yeah . . ."

Erin hopped up on the stage, and Les scrambled after her. Erin squealed and hugged me. "You are so cool, Lily! I had no idea you had it in you! We told the chaperones we were with the band, and they let us in, raving about how great you guys were."

"Um, thanks." I kept my eye on Les as I hugged Erin.

The second she let go of me, Les grabbed my wrist and hauled me against him, giving me a hug. "You were great," he whispered against my ear. "You look so hot." He let go of me and raised his voice. "I can't wait to see what you look like in your dress for the semi next week."

My cheeks heated up and I glanced at Rafe. He was scowling at Les.

Les grinned at him. "You must be Rafe."

"You must be Les."

Neither of them offered to shake hands, which was good because Rafe looked like he wanted to throw Les off the stage.

"Rafe! Rafe!"

We all turned around in time to see a familiar redhead in a pair of rhinestone jeans and a black baby tee run up to the stage and hold out her arms for Rafe to pull her up.

Paige. I felt sick.

Rafe's face lit up and he grabbed her wrists and pulled her up. Then she threw her arms around him and kissed him.

And he kissed her back.

Right there.

In front of everyone.

Chapter Fifteen XOXOX

E rin was the first to react. "You jerk!" She kicked Rafe in the shin while he was still kissing Paige.

He winced and glared at Erin. "Hey! What was that for?"

"You cheating on Lily! Right in front of her!"

A look of utter confusion swept over his face. "What are you talking about?" He glanced at me, even as I inched backward, trying to disappear.

"You!" Erin screeched. "Cheating on my best friend!"

"What—" He stared at me as sudden comprehension swept over his face. "You told them—"

Paige smacked him in the chest and jerked out of his arms. "You're *dating* Lily? You swore she was in the band because your aunt forced you to let her play!"

"I'm *not* dating Lily." He tried to catch Paige's hands as she pounded at his chest, ranting at him. "Lily!"

I wanted to die. *Die.* Right there.

Les stepped up and swung his arm around my shoulder. "I'll take care of you, Lily. You're better off without him."

I was too numb to shrug him off. I just stood there.

Rafe's eyes flashed at me. "What game are you playing?" he demanded.

"Rafe!" Paige grabbed his wrist. "I can't believe you lied to me! You're a—"

"Tell her, Lily. Tell Paige the truth." He

glared at me, accusation deep in his eyes.

I swallowed. "We're not dating. We never were."

Paige froze and stared at me. "You're lying."

I didn't look at Les or Erin. I just met Rafe's angry gaze. "I'm sorry, Rafe. It was an accident, and then, well, I . . ."

Les dropped his arm off my shoulder. "He's not your boyfriend? You lied about it? Why? To try to get me to take you to the semi? You're that much of a loser?"

Erin smacked Les in the shoulder. "She's not a loser!"

Rafe ignored them both to focus on me. "He's not your boyfriend?"

I bit my lip and shook my head.

"Why'd you lie?"

"I . . ."

Everyone waited for me to come up with an explanation, but I had none. Nothing.

So I turned and ran instead.

X O X

I didn't get out of bed until Wednesday, when my mom finally realized I wasn't actually sick and forced me to go back to school. All my friends had called repeatedly, but I wouldn't take the calls when my mom banged on my door. Even *Angel* had tried to reach me.

But Rafe hadn't.

And Les hadn't.

It was horrible.

And it was even worse when I walked into homeroom and saw Erin, Val, and Delilah huddled in the corner. Whispering.

I bit my lip and sat down at my desk.

Then the chair next to me was pulled out. I looked up to see Erin sitting down next to me, then Val sat on my desk and Delilah plopped down in the chair next to me. I raised my chin and glared at them, daring them to harass me.

"So," Erin said. "We've all talked about it, and we've come to a conclusion."

They were going to ditch me now. I knew it. "I don't care." I clenched my fists under the desk, digging my fingernails into my palms.

"See, we watched you guys perform all night," Val said. "And it's pretty obvious that Rafe is in love with you."

I felt my throat tighten. "That's not funny."

"We're serious," Erin said.

I glanced at her, and my gut caught at the look on her face. "You are?"

"Yep." Delilah tapped my arm. "He's really dating that red-haired chick?"

I nodded.

"Well, that's why she kissed him then, because she could tell he was mashing on you during the show," Val said.

I stared at her. "Really?"

"Swear."

I looked around at all of them. I couldn't believe they weren't harassing me for lying. But they weren't. They were all serious and their eyes were bright. "You really . . . think he likes me?"

"As much as you like him," Erin said.

I felt my cheeks heat up, and Erin grinned. "You're so busted. Why weren't you straight up with us from the start?"

The truth tumbled out of me before I could stop it. "Because you met all these guys over break and I had no one and I felt like a loser and then it came out and I didn't know how to stop it and—" I took a deep breath. "It doesn't matter. He has a girlfriend."

Erin sighed. "Yeah. There is that."

"And Les isn't interested anymore," I said.

"Les is an idiot," Val said. "I'm glad you're not going with him. I didn't want to tell you when you were liking him, but he made some really jerky comments about you after the pool party. He's a cretin."

That didn't surprise me. "So, I guess I'm not going to the semi." I sighed. I was back to where I'd been on the first day back after my tour. But at least my friends didn't seem keen on dumping me. That was good.

They exchanged glances and I frowned. "What now?"

Val set her hand on my shoulder and gave me a firm stare. "Here's the deal, Lily. First rule of not being a loser is to not let jerky guys win. You have to go to the semi with a guy to show up both Rafe and Les."

"Yeah, like who?"

"The singer," Erin said. "We all decided he's completely cute."

"Chris?" I sat back and thought about it. "He *is* really nice."

"Do it," Val said. "You can still quadruple date with us."

I eyed them. "Maybe . . ."

Mrs. Griffith came in the room then, and everyone slid into their seats.

Erin jotted a note and slid it over to me. *You were really good Saturday night. Have you thought about finding a band to play with for real? You were cool.*

She'd underlined *cool* about six times. I traced my finger over the words. It had been fun, that was for sure. But it had been fun mostly because of Rafe.

Hadn't it?

X O X

I called Chris Thursday night. I hung up the first three times I dialed. Then I called Erin, got a pep talk, and then called him again.

He answered almost right away. "S'up?"

I cleared my throat. "Um, Chris?"

"Yeah. Who's this?"

I almost hung up again, but made myself answer. "It's Lily. From the band."

"Hey, Lil." His voice warmed up immediately. "I thought I recognized your voice. Great job Saturday night. You bailed before I could tell you."

"Yeah, um, curfew." I rushed on before he could bring up the incident with Rafe. "So anyway, I've got this semiformal dance at my school Friday night and I was wondering if you wanted to go with me." I rushed through the invite so fast I wasn't even sure he'd understand what I'd said.

"This Friday?"

"Yeah. It was the only day we could get the location we wanted. I mean, usually it's Saturday, but we picked Friday so we could have it at the Red Pines Country Club. It's owned by the dad of this girl in my class and the food will be so good and they have this great dance floor and—"

"Relax, Lily," he interrupted. "You don't need to convince *me* to hang out with you. I'm there."

I caught my breath. "Really? Just like that?"

He chuckled. "Yeah, just like that. Rafe's an idiot. I'm not. I'm definitely coming."

"Oh." I leaned back in my pillows and uncurled my fingers from the phone. "Well. That's great."

"What time does it start?"

"Eight."

He was silent for a sec, and I felt tension sliding through me. He was going to bail on me, wasn't he? "How about I meet you there?" he said. "We've got practice until eight. I'll bring my stuff and jet over and meet you."

I noticed that he didn't ask if I was going to practice. Guess I'd been fired.

Dumped by two fake boyfriends *and* fired from the band.

My lucky week. But at least I had a date for the semi. Things were looking up. Rah, rah. "Yeah, that's fine to meet me there."

"Lily? What's wrong?"

I twirled my hair around my finger. "Nothing."

"We'll have fun, I promise."

He sounded so sincere, I actually smiled. "Okay."

"Good. Be prepared to dance. I'm a great dancer."

"I'm sure I'm better," I shot back.

He laughed. "You'll just have to prove it on Friday then, okay?"

"Deal."

We hung up after that, and my elation faded almost right away. I didn't want to go with Chris. I wanted to go with Rafe.

I tossed the phone aside and stared at my JamieX poster for a while, but I couldn't stop thinking about Rafe.

So finally I got up and went downstairs to the piano.

I played Chopin for about one minute, then switched over to the music they'd played at the piano bar.

I played for an hour, until I was sweating and singing and even feeling a little better. Weird. Piano had never made me feel better about anything before. Only worse. But tonight it made me feel better, and it was all because of Rafe.

Friday night, I stood by the door at the dance, in my black dress that Mom had insisted on buying for me, watching everyone walk in and look at me: the poor loser standing by herself.

Why had I agreed to meet Chris here? How idiotic was that? It would have been much better to meet him at my house, no matter how late we were getting here. I mean, seriously, everyone was here with a date. It wasn't like I had anyone to hang out with.

Erin walked up behind me and rested her chin on my shoulder. "You said Chris was coming from practice, right?"

Relief rushed through me at the sound of her voice, and I nodded, staring at the door, grateful that she'd ditched Keith for a few minutes to hang with me. Les had quadruple dated with them, with some "ugly chick" (Erin's words) from St. Mary's. A junior, Erin had told me.

Like that made me feel better.

Les had snagged a junior at the last minute.

And I'd been stood up.

"So, I have a theory," Erin continued.

I frowned and turned toward her. "You think Rafe told Chris not to come, don't you?" I stomped my foot. "I knew it! I was thinking that, but then I thought Rafe wouldn't care enough, or that Chris was too nice to leave me hanging. But that's what happened, isn't it? That's why Chris is late? Stupid Rafe!"

She grinned. "Actually, I think Chris told Rafe he was taking you, and Rafe talked him into letting him come in Chris's place."

My heart stuttered. "Really?"

Her smile widened. "I think the reason your date is late is because Rafe is taking you and he had to rush home to get a suit."

I clutched at her arms. "Really? You *swear*? Because I'll kill you if you're wrong!"

She giggled, her eyes gleaming. "Rafe totally loves you! Anyone watching that performance could have seen that. Now that he knows you're single, he's going to make his move."

I frowned. "Les stopped liking me once he knew I was single."

"That's because Les is a dork." She reached up and tucked a stray hair back into my bun. "You look awesome. Rafe will die when he sees you."

Suddenly, a hand fell on my shoulder, and I saw Erin's eyes widen at whoever was behind me.

I immediately spun around.

It was Chris.

Disappointment surged through me as he smiled.

"Hey, Lily. You look awesome." He leaned forward and kissed me on the cheek.

I managed a smile. "You look pretty decent in a suit too." He did. His hair was all slicked back and he smelled nice. Unfortunately, he wasn't Rafe.

He held out a corsage. "For you."

I stared at the beautiful arrangement of pink roses and baby greens. "You got me flowers?"

"Of course. It's a semiformal, isn't it?" He tugged an elastic band free. "It's a wrist corsage. Hold out your hand."

I sighed as he set the flowers around my wrist. They were so pretty. I held them to my face and inhaled. They smelled great too. And Chris looked hot. So why did I feel like I was going to cry?

He threw his arm around my shoulder and started walking toward the dance floor. "I think you need a dance."

"I don't feel like dancing."

"Tough." He released me and started dancing. "Come on, piano girl. Shake that booty like you do when you're playing the keyboard."

I felt my cheeks heat up even as I grinned. "Shut up."

"Never." He grabbed my hand and yanked me toward him. "Dance with me, Lily." He wrapped his arm around my waist and put his mouth close to my ear so I could hear him over the music. "I know I'm not Rafe, but we can still have fun tonight, can't we?"

I jerked my head back to look at him. He knew I liked Rafe?

He laughed as if I'd said the words out loud. "Everyone knows," he yelled over the music. "That was a great scene last weekend after our gig. Totally threw him for a loop. Good one!"

I felt some of my tension ease away. "Really?"

"Heck yeah!" He grabbed my hand and

spun me around. "It's good for Rafe to get knocked around a little. It was hilarious to watch his face!" he shouted. "He's been moping around at school all week, which he deserves for choosing Paige over you."

I grinned and started dancing when he let go of me. "Thanks for going with me!"

"Are you kidding? It was awesome to watch Rafe's face when I told him tonight that you'd asked me."

I felt my heart stutter. "What did he say?"

Chris threw his arms over his head and started doing this really weird hip-shaking thing. "Nothing! He just looked shocked! It was great! He was so jealous I thought he was going to punch me!"

"Really?" That was the best news ever!

Chris leaned forward and yelled in my ear. "Lily, he's still going out with Paige. Give up on him."

I grimaced. He was right. "I know," I shouted back. "I'm over him."

"Good! Maybe then you'll notice me!"

I gaped as Chris winked at me and then spun around to the music.

Chris and me? Hmm.

I started dancing for real.

Chapter Sixteen

Chris and I stopped to grab a drink after about an hour. He headed off to get a couple of waters and I snagged a seat at one of the tables, still breathing heavily from the dancing. He was a great dancer, and he made me laugh, and the night was going way better than I'd expected.

I'd barely thought about Rafe at all.

I leaned back in my seat and scanned the room. I wrinkled my nose when I noticed Les just off to the right, standing by himself and watching the dance floor.

His face darkened when he noticed a gorgeous blond girl slow dancing with another guy as they swirled past him. He reached out and grabbed her arm, tugging her free.

I leaned forward to listen as the girl glared at Les. "Leave me alone, Les."

"You're my date," he yelled over the music. "Not his!"

I grinned as she rolled her eyes. "Well, I'm ditching you. Be a man and get over it."

"But—"

She held up her hand to silence him, then she spun off with her new guy.

Les whirled around, saw me, and I immediately wiped my grin off my face. He scowled, then noticed I was alone and walked over to me. "So, you want to dance or what?"

I nodded at Chris, who was walking up behind him. "Got a date." I couldn't help but snicker at the sour look on Les's face as he sized up Chris.

I saw the moment Chris recognized him.

His eyes narrowed a fraction, then he broke into a broad grin and slapped Les on the shoulder. "Man, am I glad you were too stupid to hang on to her. Your loss, buddy." He set my drink in front of me and rested his hand on my shoulder.

"You're really with her?" Les asked.

Chris nodded and sat down next to me, draping his arm over the back of my chair. "See ya," he said purposefully.

Les glared at us both and then stalked off. I burst into laughter as soon as he was out of earshot. "That was too funny!"

Chris grinned and held out my drink for me. "That guy's an idiot. I can't believe you were going to go with him. Let me guess, football player?"

"Lacrosse," I said as I took the water. "He knows nothing about music."

"As I said, idiot." He slanted a look at me. "Is that what you're into? Lacrosse players?"

"Why? Are you one?" I realized then that I knew very little about Chris, other than that he was nice to me.

He shook his head and shoved the sleeves of his blazer up his forearms. "Singer all the way. That bug you?"

"No way. It's great." I took a sip of my water and enjoyed the sight of Les lurking by the punch bowl, looking annoyed. "Just don't ask me to ever sing with you."

He raised his brows. "You think you can't sing?"

"I *know* I can't sing."

"Everyone can sing. You just gotta practice."

I frowned. "No, really, I can't."

He snorted in disbelief. "Sure you can. You just have to try."

I sighed as I thought of Rafe and how he'd accepted my lack of singing ability. How he suffered from the same thing. He got me. Didn't want me to change. I held up my hand as Chris continued to push on the singing thing. "Let it go, okay?"

He fell silent for a moment, and then I felt

bad. I mean, he'd been super nice and all. It wasn't his fault he wasn't Rafe. "You want to dance?"

He grinned, and his shoulders relaxed. "Definitely."

I let him grab my hand and tug me to my feet. I loved to dance, and I was going to get over Rafe and have fun with Chris, end of story.

We were standing on my front steps after the dance.

Me.

Chris.

In the dark.

He shoved his hands in his pockets, his face sort of shadowed by the porch light. "So, I had a ton of fun tonight. Thanks for inviting me."

I grinned. "Thanks for coming. You're an awesome dancer."

"So are you." He slipped his hand out of his pocket and brushed his fingers over my dress. "This looks great on you."

My throat suddenly tightened up at the look on his face. "Um, thanks."

He set his other hand on my waist and sort of leaned in. "Lily . . ."

Uh-oh. This was it! He was going to *kiss* me. I bent backward as he leaned closer, my heart racing. He was cute. He was nice. He liked me. I should kiss him . . . shouldn't I?

I should. Rafe was out of my life. He wasn't going to be my first kiss and that was the way it was.

I lifted my face and waited as Chris leaned in . . . closer . . . almost there . . . then I turned my head and let his lips hit my cheek. He made a noise of surprise and snapped his eyes open.

"I gotta go!" I spun around and raced inside and slammed the door shut before he could speak.

I ran all the way up to my room and dove onto my bed, as the reality of what had just happened hit me. I sat up in horror. What had I just done? I'd run away and slammed the door in my date's face! The one guy who was interested in me and I'd just made it impossible to ever speak to him again.

I grabbed my pillow, smashed it over my face, and screamed.

Chapter Seventeen

XOXO

The next morning, I woke up to a light knock on my door. "Lily? Are you up?"

I groaned and looked at my clock. "Mom! It's only eight thirty. On Saturday." I pulled my pillow over my head. "Let me sleep!"

"There's a car out front. I think someone is here to see you."

"What?" I scrambled to my feet as my mom opened my door and walked in. I yanked my curtain aside and jerked up the shade.

There was a black Jeep sitting in front of the house.

Rafe was in it, wearing sunglasses and his leather jacket. He was playing the drums on his steering wheel, and glancing at the house every few seconds.

I jumped back, my heart thudding wildly. "It's Rafe!"

"I know." My mom pulled my shade up. "Band practice today? Or something . . . else?"

"No, I . . ." Omigosh! He was here to take me to the audition! But why? He'd mentioned it only that one time, and we hadn't even talked and I hadn't even decided I wanted to go . . . in fact I didn't, did I? I didn't. "Tell him to go away."

She raised her brow. "A deal's a deal, Lily. You have to play in the band. Go."

"But—"

She gave me her "mom" look and walked out.

How long would he wait?

I ran to the window again and looked out.

He'd tipped back his seat and looked like he was taking a nap.

Crud!

I stepped back, my hands shaking. What should I do?

Go out there. I had to. So I could tell him to go away.

Right.

I jerked on a pair of nice pants and an audition-worthy top (forget the corduroy dress!). Not that I was going to the audition or anything. Just to keep my options open.

Then I ran into the bathroom and brushed my teeth.

Then I put on some makeup and fixed my hair. Twice.

And then I took a deep breath and ran down the stairs and out the door and down the front walk.

Rafe sat up as I slowed to a stop next to the Jeep. I couldn't see his eyes because he was wearing sunglasses.

Neither of us said anything for a minute.

Then he cleared his throat. "So, audition?"

I frowned. "Why would I want to go to the audition?" I asked, hoping he might know the answer. I sure didn't.

"Because piano's fun."

"So?"

"And you can go and play something you like. Not something classical. Make it fun."

I pressed my lips together, annoyed at the part of me that agreed with him. Piano had been different for me since I'd met Rafe. Fun. A part of me I liked again.

"You're brilliant on the piano. You deserve this break."

I felt a bubble of warmth in my chest. "Brilliant?"

"Yeah."

"Oh." I dragged my toe through the dirt. I really did want to go. On my terms. With Rafe, and without my parents or Crusty or anyone else knowing. Just us. Having fun.

Could I handle going to the audition with Rafe? Knowing we were just friends and that's all it would ever be? But, then again, he was here, even knowing that I'd lied. He didn't hate me, so why should I hate him? Why should I feel stupid around him?

"Lily?"

I took a deep breath, then I hopped into the Jeep. "We'll go check it out. I'm not saying I'm going to play or anything."

He grinned and started the engine. "Agreed."

Then he turned on the radio, pulled away from the curb, and started to sing along to JamieX.

I joined right in.

We sounded horrific together, and it was awesome.

Ninety minutes later, I was sitting next to Rafe in the back of the auditorium at NESM, listening to each musical prodigy play. I'd never heard so many talented people before, and I knew I didn't belong. But I wanted to belong. I hadn't expected to want to, but I did. So much. And I knew I was too scared to go up there.

Then Rafe leaned over, his breath warm

against my ear. "You're better."

I shook my head, gripping my fingers in my lap.

"How can you deny it? You belong up there."

"Really?" I turned to face him, throwing a challenge at him. "I'm no better than you are. If I belong up there, why aren't you up there?"

He looked startled by my comment. "Me?"

"Yeah." I propped my elbow on the seat arm. "Why not you?"

He stared at me for a moment, then shook his head. "I don't know. I never thought about it."

I cocked my head, a sudden idea forming. "I'll do it if you do it with me." I couldn't do it alone, but with Rafe, I knew I'd be able to.

His eyebrows went up. "Seriously?"

"Sure, why not? We'll play that song you wrote for the band."

"Really?" His eyebrows went even higher. "Even though you're auditioning for their classical program, not their contemporary one?"

"So? A girl can change her mind." I tensed

as the woman down front called out my name. "So? You in? The drums are already on the stage."

He met my gaze for a long moment, then stood up. "Let's go have some fun."

I grinned and hopped to my feet, excitement whirring through me. I was really going to do this, on my terms! Rafe caught my smile and he grabbed my hand. He held it all the way down to the stage and while I told the woman that I was changing my audition and that Rafe was joining me. She tried to protest, but we ignored her and did it anyway.

And then we were on stage, playing like we were the only two people in the room, as we'd done at Mueller-Fordham. It was the best music I'd ever heard or felt or played, and I knew then that music was who I was, and I loved it.

When we finished, we grinned at each other as the room applauded, and I knew it didn't matter if I got in or not. It was enough that I'd come to the audition and kicked butt. Because I had.

Lily Gardner was no longer a musical failure.

I hopped off the stage and Rafe landed next to me. He grabbed me and swept me up in a big hug. "You were brilliant."

I hugged him back. "Thanks to you! You were awesome too!"

He set me down and looked at me, his face going serious. "Lily . . ."

"Lily!" We both turned around to see my mom and Miss Jespersen hurrying down the aisle toward us.

My insides clenched. "What are *they* doing here?"

"No idea." Rafe moved next to me, settling his arm around my shoulder. "Hi, Aunt Joyce," he said cautiously. "What's up?"

But she didn't answer. She simply threw her arms around both of us and hugged us so hard I thought I was going to burst. When she let go, I thought I saw her eyes watering.

"I'm so proud of you, Lily. I knew you could do it."

I gaped at her in astonishment. Was this the same Crusty? "But I didn't play classical. Aren't you mad?"

She shook her head. "You were fantastic. How could I ask for anything more? I'll go talk to them about switching your application to the contemporary program. That's what you want, isn't it?"

I nodded instinctively before I could process the question, realizing that that's exactly what I wanted.

Then she turned to Rafe. "And you! I'm going to talk to them about you! How come you hid your talent from me? I had no idea you were that good!"

Rafe shrugged and scuffed his feet. "I was just doing my thing. I didn't think it mattered."

"Oh, Rafe, it matters. You matter." She hugged us both again, muttered something about having a chat with Rafe's mom, then hurried off to talk to the woman running the audition . . . leaving my mom standing there, her eyes bright. "Lily, darling, I hope you didn't mind, but when I saw you and Rafe drive off, I thought you might be coming here. I called Miss Jespersen and we decided to come."

I eyed her carefully, waiting for her to jump all over me for my music choice. "And?"

"I'm so proud of you."

I felt a tinge of relief. "Really?"

"You were wonderful up there, Lily." She hugged me, squeezing tight when I hugged her back. "I'm sorry I pressured you, hon. Miss Jespersen was right that we needed to give you room. I promise I'll back off and let you and Miss Jespersen make the decisions, okay?"

I snorted. "You won't be able to do that."

She looked offended for a moment, then laughed. "I'll try, okay?"

"Okay," I said, smiling back.

Miss Jespersen came running back. "Rafe! They loved you and are accepting your application, even though it's late." She beamed at both of us. "They didn't come out and say it, but I think you both will be starting NESM next year. I'm so proud!"

My mom screeched and hugged me. "I have to go call Dad. We'll all go out to celebrate tonight, including Rafe and Miss Jespersen."

She didn't wait for an answer, as she dug her phone out of her purse and rushed out of the auditorium to use it.

Miss Jespersen hugged us *again* and then hurried off to work the room, no doubt trying to cement our applications.

Our applications. As in, me and Rafe, attending NESM together. *Together.* I looked at him, and he was still looking stunned. I elbowed him.

"Earth to Rafe."

He looked at me, grinned, then grabbed my hand and tugged me down the aisle and out of the auditorium so we could talk alone. He stopped immediately in the hall outside and turned me so I was facing him.

"Are you going to come to NESM if you get in?" I asked.

"You bet I am." He ran his hand through his hair. "I can't even believe this. What an incredible opportunity." Then he looked at me. "What about you? Will you do it?"

I nodded. "I think the contemporary program would rock."

His grin widened. "So, we'll be hanging

together next semester, then. Can you put up with seeing that much of me?"

I immediately frowned and took a step back. "The bigger question is, can Paige put up with you spending that much time with me?"

His smile faded, and he got that serious look on his face again. "Okay, so I was going to tell you this earlier, but I didn't want to distract you from the audition."

Oh, here it comes. Was there any way to avoid this humiliation? "Rafe—"

"Chris told me about last night. About how you wouldn't kiss him."

My mouth dropped open. I wanted to crawl under the nearest table in embarrassment. "He *told* you?"

"Yeah." Rafe was watching me really intently. He looked tense and sort of nervous. "I was psyched when he told me."

I lifted my chin and set my hands on my hips. "Who I kiss is none of your business. Why would you care anyway? You have a girlfriend."

He shook his head, not taking his eyes off my face. "Actually, I don't. I broke up with her."

I smacked his chest. "*What?* Since when?"

"The night of the middle school dance. After you left."

I stared at him, my ears starting to get this weird buzzing. "Seriously? Why?"

"She told me she could tell I liked you from the way I looked at you during the show." He shrugged. "She was right."

I was vaguely aware of students milling by, but I couldn't drag my gaze off Rafe. "But why didn't you tell me?"

"I didn't know if you liked me."

I hit him again. "Are you an *idiot*?"

He grinned and caught my hand. "Well, you did ask Chris to the dance, not me."

"You had a girlfriend!"

"I didn't, actually." He leaned toward me, his thumb rubbing over my chin. "But you didn't kiss him. So I decided to come today."

My heart fluttered in my chest. "Maybe I just don't kiss on the first date."

"Maybe." He moved even closer, so near I could smell his toothpaste. "Do you kiss in broad daylight?"

I swallowed hard, my heart beating so fast I could feel it smashing against my chest. "Depends."

He dropped his gaze to my lips. "On what?"

"Um . . ." I couldn't remember what I was going to say.

His hand curved around my chin and he lifted my face, and then he kissed me.

Playing the piano was fun again, but it didn't begin to compare to my first kiss . . . with Rafe.

So worth waiting for.

Ready for your next first kiss?
Here's an excerpt from
Puppy Love
by Jenny Collins

So Rufus and I went to the park. I love walking with him. He's curious about everything, and he always acts as if it's the first time he's sniffed grass or heard birds or seen people on bicycles, even though he's almost ten and we go to the park just about every day. There's no way to be sad when you're walking Rufus, or any dog for that matter. They're just so happy to be outside that their happiness rubs off on you. I'm telling you, the way to get yourself feeling good again when you're sad isn't to eat a dozen chocolate chip cookies or buy some new shoes, it's to walk a dog.

And I *was* feeling better. Walking Rufus, I knew I'd be able to handle six dogs for a day. Yes, I still wished Shan could be there to do it with me, but I knew I would be okay. Six dogs isn't that many, and three of them were big. Contrary to popular belief, big dogs are a lot easier to handle than small dogs. Mostly they just like to play a little fetch and take naps. But the little ones stay active all day long. Personally, I think it's because little dogs have just as much energy as the big ones but it takes longer for them to use it up.

I was thinking of games I could play with the dogs when the squirrel made its entrance. I didn't even see it. But Rufus did. And if there's one thing Rufus can't resist, it's a squirrel. They make him crazy. And being a bear-dog, Rufus is really strong, so when he wants to run after something you have to be prepared for it, which I usually am. But for some reason my mind was somewhere else just then, so when the leash suddenly jerked me forward, I ended up falling all over myself. There I was, lying on the grass, watching Rufus's leash drag along behind him while he ran away, barking his head off.

I got up as soon as I could and ran after him, calling his name, which I knew wasn't going to help. When Rufus is chasing a squirrel, he uses his whole brain to focus on catching it. You can yell all you want to, but he won't hear you. I yelled anyway, mainly so everyone watching me would think I was trying to do something to stop him.

You'd think the squirrel would go to the first tree it saw and climb it, right? Well, this one didn't. It just kept running, with Rufus behind it and me behind Rufus. I tried to keep up with them, but let's face it, four legs are always going to be faster than two.

They got farther and farther away from me until finally they reached the edge of what we call the Dog Bowl—this part of the park where there's a dip between some small hills. A lot of people bring their dogs there because it's a great place to toss balls and let the dogs run around together without them getting in the way of the rollerbladers, joggers, and people pushing strollers through the park.

Rufus and the squirrel disappeared over the edge of the Dog Bowl. Then I heard Rufus stop barking, which was weird. When he's after a squirrel he barks until you get him away from it. I don't know what I thought might have happened to Rufus, but I suddenly got scared. What if he was hurt? Or maybe the squirrel had friends. Lots of friends, like a little squirrel army. It's stupid, I know. I never said that I'm always rational, okay? I'm a worrier.

When I reached the edge of the Dog Bowl I looked down, half expecting to see Rufus surrounded by crazy warrior squirrels. Instead, he was sitting beside a guy who was holding the end of his leash and patting Rufus on the head. The guy was probably not much older than me, and my first thought was, great—it would be just my luck that he would end up being in my high school. He was looking around, and I could tell he was trying to figure out what moron let her dog run away. Being the moron in question, I walked down the hill toward him, trying to think of something to say so I wouldn't look as dumb as I felt.

When Rufus saw me, he looked up with his big brown eyes and started wagging his tail, which he always does when he knows he's done something bad. He knows it's hard to be angry at him when he looks like that. Usually it works. But I was pretty mad at him, so I tried to ignore his adorableness.

"Not this time, mister," I told him.

"Sounds like you're in trouble, buddy," the guy said to Rufus. He had a really nice, calming voice. The boy, I mean, not Rufus. He turned and handed me the leash. "I take it this isn't his first offense?" he said.

"He was on squirrel patrol," I answered, taking the leash. For a second, our hands touched.

The guy nodded. "You've got to watch out for those squirrels," he said, scratching Rufus behind the ears. "I hate to tell you this, but that's a losing battle."

I laughed. I couldn't tell if he was talking to me or Rufus. "Thanks for catching him," I said.

"No problem." He looked at me and smiled, and that's when I noticed his eyes. They were dark brown, just like Rufus's. His hair was a dark golden-brown, and it fell in his face a little bit. *He's kind of cute,* I thought. Then I realized I was staring at him, and I looked away. I didn't want him to think I was an incompetent dog walker *and* all into him.

"We've got to go," I said, tugging at Rufus so that he got up and followed me. "Thanks again."

I walked back up the hill. Part of me wanted to look back and see if the guy was watching me, but I just kept going. For some reason, if he wasn't watching me, I didn't want to know. So I kept my eyes on Rufus and walked until I couldn't see over the edge of the Dog Bowl. Then I breathed a sigh of relief.

"Thanks for making me look stupid," I told Rufus. "And you had to do it in front of the cutest guy you could find, didn't you?"

Rufus looked up at me and wagged his tail. This time I couldn't resist him. I knelt down, rubbed his ears, and kissed him on the nose. "I know," I said. "You can't help it."

He licked my face.

"Dog kisses," I said, giving him a hug. "The best kind."

I slipped my hand through the handle of his

leash and wrapped it around my wrist. If any more squirrels crossed our path, I'd be ready for them. "Come on," I said to Rufus. "Let's go home."

READ ALL OF THE BOY-CRAZY BOOKS IN THE FIRST KISSES SERIES!

First Kisses: Trust Me

Counselor-in-training Jess finds out her trust partner is also her long-time nemesis (with beautiful blue eyes) Sean Reed, the most untrustworthy person she knows. But will Jess trust her instincts or fall in love with him anyway?

First Kisses: The Boyfriend Trick

When the pressure of being a piano prodigy gets to be too much for Lily, her music teacher asks her to join a rock band in order to rediscover her passion. What Lily doesn't plan on is feeling passionate about Rafe, the band's drummer!

First Kisses: Puppy Love

Allie can't wait to run a doggy day care at her mom's shop, Perfect Paws, until she has to watch over mega-snob Megan's horrible poodle, who leads her into trouble—and the arms of the boy who works at the local shelter, Jack.

First Kisses: It Had to Be You

Fashionable, girly Emma may be an expert at giving other people romantic advice, but when it comes to boys right under her nose—like her cute next-door neighbor Kyle— Emma's completely at a loss.

First Kisses: Playing the Field

Trisha practices soccer with this really cool sophomore Graham, a boy who finally treats her like one of the guys. But are they starting to fall for each other, or is he just playing around?

First Kisses: The Real Thing

School photographer Hayley has a "camera crush" on football hottie Flynn, who happens to be her sister's new boyfriend. But are her feelings more than that? Could this be the real thing?

HarperTempest
An Imprint of HarperCollinsPublishers

www.harperteen.com